To: Sheri

Merry Christmas, 2015!

Rick Cornell
12/15

"I Am That Fool", Rick Cornell's first novel (2014), was a Next Generation Indie Book Award finalist, "Best New Novelist, Under 80,000 Words". Its cover also took second place in the 2015 "ABC Book Cover Contest" sponsored by LRP Printing (LeRue Press).

Praise for "I Am That Fool"

"A page-turning, exciting novel by a new voice in the legal thriller genre.... Fans of Grisham should not miss "I Am That Fool."
Gary S. Roen of Midwest Book Review

"This...story...is thrilling as well as unbelievably realistic! .... If you enjoy legal drama like I do, check this one out!"
Glenda Bixler, "Book Reader's Heaven"

"A wonderful legal thriller [and] I don't normally care for legal thrillers."
Gayle Pace, "Books, Reviews, etc."

On www.internetradiopros.com:

"This is an excellent book. Once you start reading it, you will not put it down, except maybe for dinner or drinks."
Jack Drucker, host of "John Austin's Book Club"

RICK CORNELL

LeRue Books
Reno, Nevada

2051
Copyright ©2015 by Rick Cornell All rights reserved.

Produced in the United States of America. No part of this book may be used or reproduced, in any manner whatsoever, performed, or copied in any form without written permission except in the case of brief quotations embodied in critical articles and reviews. For information, contact LeRue Press.

Order additional copies in e-book format or print
LeRue Press
280 Greg St.
Reno, NV 89502.
www.lrpnv.com

This novel is a work of fiction. Names, characters, places, and incidents either are the product of the author's imagination or are used fictitiously. Except for obvious historical figures, any resemblance to actual persons, living or dead, businesses, companies, events, or locales is entirely coincidental.

Cover art and illustration created by Jim Zlokovich
Author's photograph by Robert Callaghan
Edited by Kathi Kimbriel

ISBN 978-1-0938814-14-3

First Edition, 2015

10 9 8 7 6 5 4 3 2 1

ACKNOWLEDGEMENTS

Way more people to acknowledge than with "I Am That Fool"; but then, a lot more thought and care went into this novel than into "I Am That Fool." Discovering how much I don't know forever amazes me!

To my beta readers: H. Louise Bernstone; Becky Earl; Nebojsa Bikic (who gave me Ana's great line in ch. XX, after consulting with his Serbian mother!); Leslie Schuh; Pris Robichaud; Becky Kyle (beta reader of the storyboard); and Tuesday Lynch. Thank you, one and all, for your input – all of which made it into the novel!

To my artist and friend, Jim Zlokovich, for another inspired cover. I love how much it says, and so economically!

To my early beta readers, who saw the flaws in my storytelling technique and inspired me to correct them before they got out of control: Jim Burk; and my incomparable son, Jon Cornell.

To Google, for helping me change the original names of some of the characters: Esperanza Gomez, a Colombian porn queen, to Esperanza Lopez; Fred Duckett, the long-time voice of the Houston Astros, to Fred Dockett; and Ana Matich, a B-movie actress from the 1960's, to Ana Katich.

  To my editor, Kathi Kimbriel, who taught me so much in so little time and whose advice hopefully helped me to elevate this novel from "promising" to something far greater than that!

  And finally, to Jan Hermsen and Lenore Halfide of LeRue Press, for helping me in so many ways with both this novel and with "I Am That Fool"!

        Rick Cornell
        September, 2015
        Cornell.Rick804@gmail.com

2051

Rick Cornell

I

December 16, 2050. Law students had finished all of their final exams at Cornell Law School. Future well-to-do lawyers of America did not include anyone who would start post-school life with the typical mid-21st century median of $500,000 of student loan debt. But for students at Ivy League colleges such as Cornell, that was not the issue. For those select few, who had the backing of trust funds and the luxury simply of concentrating on the law, mid-December meant a break from all of those mega-hours of studying and law pounding. And for the select few of the few students lucky enough to enroll in Professor Fred Dockett's Trial Practice class, that meant the famous, semester-ending cocktail party at the Professor's brownstone, 10.4 miles off of campus.

Famous for two reasons: First, the "cocktails" in question consisted of analogues of "not yet illegal, but some day guaranteed to put you in prison for at least 10 years unless Pfizer or Merck markets it first" drugs that the DEA hadn't yet figured out from the Professor's private stash, designed to expand one's mind into the genius realm. Second, the Professor did his guided tour through one of the few 18th Century brownstones left in the country, so that the students might better understand the genius of this legal guru.

Going up the stairs with the 100-year-old refinished pure mahogany bannisters and steps, one could see the focus of the home: The Professor's Den. Upon entry into the den, one could not miss the framed certificates of Professor Dockett's video game "career." Nobody in the country played "Final Fantasy 24" faster than he, and Fred Dockett had proof. The holder of the second place certificates undoubtedly approximated half of Dockett's age. And that youngster certainly had not trained his brain to think as fast as the "Windows 20"-fueled computer.

Inside of the den, the inquisitive minds could see enough exotic e-Cuban cigars and smell enough black cherry-flavored smoke to answer their semester-long speculations: What was the Professor's tobacco or tobacco-substitute of choice?

Up the next set of old wooden stairs to the pure mahogany-encased master bedroom on the third floor, or up the dumbwaiter from the old servant's quarters in the basement to the third floor entry, careful student observers would see evidence of Dockett's presence, but nobody else's. Thus, the semester-long mystery of whether the Professor had a girlfriend – or for that matter, a boyfriend -- would remain exactly that.

But what they couldn't miss in the master bedroom closet –especially with the Professor bragging about them in class – were the suits. Bright polyester monotone suits, from rose to lavender, and all pastel rainbow shades in between, with matching patent leather shoes and matching handkerchiefs. And organized in his closet by colors of the rainbow to boot. Between the suits, accessories and the pencil-thin mustache, the thin, short and dapper Fred Dockett could never be mistaken for anyone else in the country.

But when the students looked in the bedroom, closet and adjoining bathroom, their semester-long speculations came to an end on one vital subject: The Professor did not have a toupee that looked like a shedding raccoon. No mannequin heads on site portended that. The Professor simply had a bad comb-over. Professor Fred Dockett, the most famous trial lawyer in the country, had all that money and nothing but a life of bad hair days. The man was a true mid-21st century eccentric.

After receiving all the fawning admiration, the Professor announced it was time for the festivities to begin. Time for the injection of RLX-22-AJH-4C, the newest cocktail designed to create the gateway for usage of 20% more brain space. The drug that would finally cure Alzheimer's, or aging, or dementia, or writer's block. Or maybe all four – unless Big Pharm got to the DEA first.

But for Professor Dockett, the drug-induced cocktail party meant another opportunity to use "the Socratic Method" on young people, conditioned to hang on his every word, on a subject that would not appear on any final exam but might prove more relevant than anything he had taught them.

"August 31, 2049. Do you remember where you were when you heard the news?"

Student #1, the "coat and tie guy" due to his daily preppy wear, volunteered: "Yeah, in Con Law class, Professor."

Dockett chuckled that sardonic chuckle of his. "Constitutional Law, eh? How deliciously ironic…."

Student #2, ever the joker with the bright red hair, responded, "I heard it from the News Babe who does the afternoon news on Fox News. Why else do you suppose I watch Fox News?"

In a droll, eye-roll of a voice, Dockett responded, "What other reason could there possibly be?"

Everybody laughed. But then Student #3, the female Asian destined someday to be an appellate judge, asked, "Which person, Professor? Are you talking about the wife of the Secretary of Agriculture? Or the Under-Secretary of

Agriculture? Or perhaps the Deputy Director of the Bureau of Land Management? Or are you referencing the wife of the Secretary of the Interior?"

Coat-and-tie guy interrupted. "I'm sure the Professor is talking about the Chief of the U.S. Forest Service!"

"No," replied Dockett, "I'm talking about all five. I mean, they all got it within half an hour of each other, right? Does it matter which one you heard about first?"

Student #4, the female blonde conservative idealist, chimed in: "Yeah, it matters. The Department of Agriculture Secretary's wife was the first to die. If the Department of Homeland Security had realized that we are just as prone to domestic terrorism as to foreign, they could have put a stop to it immediately and kept the body count to one."

"And how were they supposed to do that?" queried the red-haired joker. "Who would have thought that Amazon.com robots, delivering food in the afternoon, would be weapons of terror?"

"The people who hatched the plot and created the fake robots, obviously," rejoined Ms. Conservative Idealist. "What gets me is the Department of Homeland Security has such a handle on everybody in this country; how did these people slip through the cracks?"

Professor Dockett interrupted the gab session: "When you live in a society with a lot of displaced and disaffected people, there are a lot of cracks to slip through, don't you think? I mean, if the NSA (National Security Agency) keeps tabs on people through their voice-activated e-mails, and the people designing the Amazon.com attack robots are too poor to afford that technology so they communicate over years by snail mail, then what is the NSA supposed to do?"

Student #5, one of the campus left-wingers and Straight-A students, chimed in: "As usual, the Professor is on it.

Look at all of them. Chronically unemployed farm workers; thank you, global warming. Get your corn and your wheat from the breadbaskets of the world, Canada and Russia. Unemployed miners. Unemployed ranchers. Unemployed frackers. Unemployed auto workers. All over the country. A lot of people pissed off at the federal government, that's for sure. And for good reason. We allowed the means of food retail distribution to be controlled by one corporation -- Amazon.com."

The Blonde Conservative Idealist responded: "Well, what do you expect? Amazon.com was the only corporation that had figured out how to prevent identity theft. And with people losing billions of dollars to identity theft each year, people have to eat. So,..."

Mr. Campus Left-winger continued the rant: "So the terrorists take out Amazon, and a lot of people starve. A brilliant move. Farmers markets, hydroponic stores and quickie-marts can get people only so far. Congress does all of these financial sequesters so that we can bankroll the military and corporations overseas, and who takes it in the neck? The little guys. The little guys who have had enough!"

"Okay," said Dockett, controlling the flow of conversation. "But how do you defend the accused? Is your defense that society made them do it?"

"Professor," replied the future appellate judge, "With all due respect, I don't think even you could defend any of those people. I mean, a trial in the Thomas & Mack Center in Las Vegas, 58 defendants, 18,000 people in the gallery cheering on the prosecution, wide screen monitors all over the place, jurors so far away they couldn't even see the defendants – How can you possibly get a fair trial under those circumstances?"

"An 'A' for you, my dear!" exclaimed Dockett to his minion, eager for recognition. "But once the FBI got the DNA and the NSA got the clues together and some of the people started confessing and pointing fingers, how could you defend the charges? How could all those snitches be lying? Don't you think there are some crimes that simply should be indefensible? Some crimes where society just has to find guilt and the strongest punishment possible, no matter what?"

"Absolutely!" said the Blonde Conservative Idealist.

"Absolutely not!" countered Mr. Coat-and-Tie Guy. "The Constitution grants a fair trial for all. When we start carving out exceptions to that, we lose the meaning of the Sixth Amendment! Does anyone remember studying the Lindbergh baby kidnapping case, or the Ethel Rosenberg case from the 20th Century? A rush to judgment by the inflamed public meant execution of innocent people! How is that right?"

"And an 'A' for you as well, my friend!" stated Dockett, patting Coat-and-Tie Guy on the shoulder. "And let me ask you," said Dockett, as he looked right at the Blonde Conservative Idealist, "With the criminals caught, having their trials, and being sentenced to death, wasn't that enough? Did we really need 'The Super Patriot Act of 2049'?"

On that one subject the Professor and all of his students could agree: No, not really. But Congress had a 2% approval rating in 2049. The two-party political system simply didn't work any longer, and hadn't for decades. People didn't know what to do about Congress, except complain about it, and in increasingly dangerous, rhetorical tones. The federal politicians knew the drill: They needed to set aside their differences and put their country first. Or if they couldn't do that, then they needed to set aside their differences and raise that 2% rating.

Following his personal drama with his father, Ryan in the year 2015, Beau Browne led a relatively quiet, uneventful life. He served as the Pastor of the local Congregational Church, with his wife a loyal leader and supporter of church activities. Beau enjoyed the reputation as a well-liked, popular and respected man in his community. He had spoken at many a Governor's prayer breakfast throughout the years. As he edged near retirement, Beau and his wife essentially lived off the legacy left to him by his long-deceased mother, Tania Browne.

One night in early January of 2051 Beau couldn't sleep. He got up from the parsonage where he and his wife lived, and walked to the nearby Congregational sanctuary. As he went to the front pew for some prayer time, he spotted a man sleeping in a nearby pew. *This is odd; how did this man get into the church?*

"Sir," said Beau, as he gently shook the man, "I'm sorry, but I can't have you sleeping in my church. There are homeless shelters for that, and I can show you where they are."

The man slowly awoke, and Pastor Browne immediately recognized him.

"Wait a minute! Adam? Adam Kolkoski?"

"Hi, Pastor Browne."

"Adam, what are you doing here? Weren't you just here last Sunday?"

"Pastor Browne, I haven't slept for days. My body aches."

"Oh, you poor man! Here, let's go over to the Fellowship Hall and have some coffee together."

The two proceeded to the Fellowship Hall. As the coffee maker brewed the harsh-tasting mud, designed to awaken any Rip Van Winkle of the world, Pastor Browne asked the obvious line of questions: "Adam, is this the first time you've been sleeping in my sanctuary?"

"No, Pastor Browne, I've been doing that for two weeks now."

"Why?"

At this point, with Adam now fully awake thanks to the bitter swill, Kolkoski launched into his story:

"When I was a young man, 45 years ago, I went through a breakup with my long-time girlfriend. I was depressed for weeks. I thought I had nothing to live for. I finally went on the Yahoo.com adult romance chat room website."

Beau asked, "The Yahoo.com adult romance chat room? I've never heard of it. Is it still around?"

Adam replied: "Not any more, thanks to my case and a bunch of others like mine that happened at the same time. They shut it down after this. But in its day this chat room was as popular as Match.com, Christian Mingle and E-Harmony.

Before long, I struck up a conversation with a female who claimed she was 14-years-old."

Beau interrupted, " Well, but didn't you know right off the bat that it was a police sting?"

Adam replied, "Yeah, I thought the situation was weird. But this was an *adult* romance chat room. As far as I knew, this wasn't a place where pedophiles were hanging around. So, it didn't seem to be the kind of website the police would be interested in infiltrating.

And the young woman wasn't talking in the slang that I thought was typical for teenagers back then. She used phrases like 'I don't want to be *preggo*.' I thought kids hadn't used that phrase in ten years or more. I thought she might have been an adult, pretending to be a teenager.

So, for that reason, I asked the young lady for a photograph. And right away, she instant messaged me this photo of a gorgeous young woman riding a horse. Well, I was immediately turned on. From the photo, my guess was the girl was about 19-years- old, pretending to be 14 in order to play into some kind of weird sexual fantasy. I didn't care about the weird fantasy; I just wanted to know more about this young lady if she really was 19. I wanted to meet her, to see how old she was and if she really was the girl in the picture. So we agreed to meet at a place downtown.

Adam talked more slowly and bitterly: "I was all excited, like only a stupid 21-year-old boy can be. I showed up with three condoms and a hotel key in my wallet, just in case she happened to be a 19-year-old, willing to have sex with me. But instead, this gorgeous blonde woman who looked to be about 25-years-old approached me. This obviously wasn't the girl in the photograph; this was someone older and even more beautiful. I didn't care. I thought I had hit pay dirt."

Adam then went more quickly through his story, as though he had told it a thousand times before and really didn't want to tell it a thousand-and-first, but had to:

"So, I approached her and showed her the key to the hotel room. The next thing I sensed were my hands being cuffed behind my back. The undercover detective, whom I didn't see behind me, arrested me on charges of using the Internet to lure a minor child into a sexual act."

"Wait a minute!" Cried Pastor Browne, shaking his head. "If I understand your story correctly, there never was a minor child involved in this at any time, and you thought you were going to have sex with a beautiful 20-something-year-old blonde?"

Even now, Adam had a tough time making it through this part of the true story: "Yeah, although as it turned out, the gorgeous 20-something-year-old blonde was actually a decoy, a probation officer, since the police detective later said in court they didn't want to use an explorer scout and 'risk liability.'

So, I was booked into state court. And shortly after my arrest the state supreme court ruled that Internet luring couldn't be based on a case where no child actually existed, but the charge of attempted luring of a minor child could, if the defendant genuinely believed he was actually luring a minor child."

"Wait a minute!" Pastor Browne exclaimed again. "Do you mean to tell me that if someone on a jury thought you were intending to have sex with a minor, even though you say you always thought the girl was an adult, even though the photo and the decoy led you to believe she was an adult, and even though the undercover officer was in fact an adult, you would be guilty of attempting to lure a minor child into a sexual act via the Internet?"

"Yeah," replied Adam. "Did you ever read Orwell's '1984'? I'm telling you, this country has had the 'Thought Police' for the past 50 years. Orwell was right on the money, though his theory might have been off by 20 years or so."

"But that's ridiculous!" replied Pastor Browne. "If the police detectives are supplying pictures over the Internet in an adult romance chat room of a late-teenaged, beautiful girl, and presenting an even better looking blonde, twenty-something-year-old as a decoy, isn't that entrapment?"

"That's what I thought," replied Adam with even more bitterness. "That's why I went to trial, even though the prosecution offered me a gross misdemeanor. I should have taken the deal. I didn't believe my lawyer when she told me it's not entrapment if law enforcement 'merely supplies me with the opportunity.' Check this out: The way the concept of 'entrapment' was explained to the jury? I would have had to be born without original sin and the government would have had to implant original sin in me, in order for it to be entrapment! So, based on that definition, the jurors didn't believe my claim of entrapment. But they also didn't believe my claim that I never thought I was communicating with a minor. They found me guilty of attempted luring of a minor child."

"That's terrible!" said Beau. "But that doesn't explain why you're sleeping in the sanctuary of my church!"

Adam went on, with his voice displaying even more, increasing bitterness as he went through the next part of his true story: "Here's the problem. The judge granted me probation. I took every sex offender therapy class required. I was honorably discharged from probation. I never got into trouble with the law again after that. But it didn't matter.

Under the Adam Walsh Act, I am rated as a level III sex-offender, and I am required to register with the Department of Public Safety as a 'Level Three'. A level III sex-offender can never get off the registry, and can never be downgraded to level II or level I. That means since 2018, every neighbor, every employer, every nearby business and every school in the town where I live, has to be advised that I am one convicted of a sex offense involving a minor child. All that matters is the name of the crime I was convicted of. The facts of my case, and the fact that no minor child was ever involved, are irrelevant. The facts that I successfully completed all sex therapy classes and never came close to "reoffending" again? Also irrelevant. Under the law I am permanently tattooed with 'CM,' standing for 'Child

Molester,' all the way to my grave. I have committed the crime that keeps on unforgiving. I am a monster."

Adam started to cry, but soldiered on: "I tried, Pastor Browne. Believe me, I tried. For years I tried. But I could not find a job anywhere that would last more than six months, before an employer would fire me due to the hassles in employing a 'CM.' Everywhere I went I was harassed. I was ridiculed. I was evicted from more apartments without cause than you can imagine. People have beaten me up emotionally. A few over the years have spit on me. More have scorned me.

Under the law I cannot get the arrest sealed ever, because attempted Internet luring is deemed a sexual offense."

Beau was even more outraged. "Oh, come now. Surely the Governor would grant you a pardon for a case like this, wouldn't he?"

Adam snorted in disgust: "Hah! Are you kidding me? Does anyone really think the Governor would ever grant a pardon to a convicted sex offender? That is what you call political suicide! People don't vote for a governor so that he can show some mercy to a CM!"

Beau found this story even more difficult to comprehend. "Surely someone must have challenged this law! It sounds all wrong!"

Adam's bitter cynicism continued. "Of course they did. The ACLU challenged it. I thought when the ACLU filed their lawsuit I might get some relief. But I lost all hope when the Supreme Court of the United States ("SCOTUS") upheld the Adam Walsh law."

Indeed, that did happen. The SCOTUS upheld Adam Walsh on the grounds that community notification wasn't "punishment." Yes, our SCOTUS believed that being emotionally beaten up without provocation, ridiculed, continuously fired without cause, continuously evicted without cause, and just generally scorned for the rest of one's life, every day until death, wasn't "punishment." Adam Kolkoski had seriously contemplated suicide, and took to sleeping in the church because, due to the latest job termination, he faced homelessness and joblessness.

Beau's outrage turned to compassion. Adam Kolkoski needed help, and Beau Browne was going to help him. Beau offered to take Adam into the spare bedroom of his parsonage, and offered him a job as the church's janitor.

Adam's eyes welled up with even more tears. It had been so long since anyone had shown Adam any act of kindness that he didn't know what to say at first. Finally, he hugged Pastor Browne and thanked him profusely.

Beau Browne had just managed to commit the biggest mistake of his life.

On September 5, 2049 Senator John O'Keefe of Massachusetts, the head of the Senate Homeland Security Committee, called for an emergency meeting with Rep. Joey "Rad" Radley of Mississippi, the head of the House Homeland Security Committee, during the summer break.

"Look," said O'Keefe, in his patrician Brahman accent. "I don't like interrupting my sailing trip in Hyannis Port, any more than you like interrupting the Biloxi Seafood Festival during your vacation, but this is serious. We have to do something. We have to come up with new law."

"Why?" Retorted Radley, in his lilting southern accent. "Why do we always need new law? What's the matter with the old law?"

"Because people in this country want action. They need to know that we are on top of this. They need to know that we can come up with something that will ensure that '831' will never happen again."

"What? Are you suggesting that we trod out that old political punching bag of global warming again?" Asked a slightly disgusted Radley. "We've been kicking that old can around the block for decades now. Look, the people in my state, and throughout the south, just aren't going to go for that. They never have, and they never will. You can commission all the studies on global warming you want. They just aren't going to buy into it."

"Even with the expanding coastlines and shrinking beaches at Waveland and at Bay Saint Louis?"

Radley snorted. "Oh, come on, now. That's an old wives tale spread by you old wives who think you know more than we do. No, global warming is not going to sell to my people."

O'Keefe felt frustration, but not as much as would have existed had Radley not been saying the same thing over and over again for more than ten years. O'Keefe responded:

"All right. Well, the obvious reform, other than addressing global warming and getting British Petroleum out of Mississippi, Louisiana and Texas – which I agree will never happen in our lifetimes – is farm supports. Our terrorists include a bunch of farm workers who have been unemployed for way too long. We need to reinstitute farm supports for these people, so that they can get back to work."

Radley wasn't about to agree with O'Keefe. "And so long as we have this financial sequester going on, it isn't happening, Senator. And you know that. Look, we haven't had a balanced budget since 1999. And with all of these corporations pulling out of the USA and going to countries where they won't be taxed so heavily, we're not ever going to have a balanced budget. And with the military in "Sunnistan", Iran, Afghanistan, Kurdistan, Turkey, Uzbekistan, Libya, Egypt, Kuwait, Dubai, Saudi Arabia, United Arab Emirates, Sudan, Liberia, Nigeria, Somalia, Indonesia, Germany, South Korea, Ukraine, Georgia, Croatia, Japan, and God knows where else, we have to cut the budget somewhere. And farm supports is one area that gets cut. That's the deal. Besides, why do we want to encourage these terrorists? Give them what they want? What do you think they're going to do then? And why on earth would we negotiate with them? Destroy them, I say! Wipe them out like the cockroaches they are! Get out 'the Raid'!"

O'Keefe sighed. As much as he disagreed with Radley, he could see that he wasn't going to get anywhere with the old coot. But he also knew that they had to come up with something. The good people of the USA demanded it.

And then O'Keefe had the brainstorm.

"All right. So what if we respond like this: What if we pass into law what we will call 'The Super Patriot Act of 2049'?"

Radley tilted his head. "What are you getting at?"

"Well, look," responded O'Keefe. "Based on the profiling the FBI did of the criminals involved in 831, it appears that a good number of them had felony convictions. And it looks like far too many of them learned their computer skills, that enabled them to put together their conspiracy without the FBI and the NSA being on to them, while they were in prison."

"Yeah, so?"

O'Keefe went on. "So, what we do is we expand the definition of the crime of treason to include 'anybody who harbors an enemy of the State.' What I'm getting at is that law will keep these criminals from living together and congregating in the free world, where they will share information, or at least deter them from doing that. The punishment for treason is mandatory life imprisonment, you know."

Radley thought about that and mused, "Well, I see your point. Yes, the public will go for that, I'm sure. It's not like convicted felons have a lobby to gum up the works, or anything. But I do see one problem."

"What?"

Radley responded, "The Super Patriot Act? Really? Doesn't that sound kind of cartoonish to you?"

O'Keefe snorted, "No more than 'Fat Man and Little Boy' dropped on Nagasaki at the end of World War II, or labeling the leaders of Al Qaeda by a deck of cards and the "weapons of mass destruction" in Iraq. You know, Americans like sound bytes and love cartoons. They always have!"

Radley went on. "Okay, you're right about that. But I see another problem. It seems to me that to be able to define who 'an enemy of the State' is with any precision will take months of hearings and comments, speech and debate, and delay. We can't afford delay. I mean, 2%? We dilly dally around any more on this issue of national security, and we're going to be at .2%!"

O'Keefe responded, "For once we agree on something! Okay, Rad, so here's what we do: We put in the amended law that the Department of Justice is delegated the responsibility of defining who 'an enemy of the State' is. After all, they are the ones who should be at the forefront of defending national security from domestic terrorists, don't you think?"

Rad Radley smiled a big smile. "Of course, John! What a public relations coup! All right, we hold a quick hearing on this, we get the Attorney General on board with this, and we have our new law!"

Had there actually been any speech and debate on the Super Patriot Act of 2049, undoubtedly some contrarian (probably that blasted goofball Senator from Minnesota or Vermont; Minnesota and Vermont always seemed to have a string of blasted contrarian, goofball Senators) would have pointed out the following:

1. As of 2049, the United States of America had been the most heavily incarcerated country in the world for decades. And the Corrections Corporation of America ("CCA") privately owned all of the federal prisons by that time, although the Federal Government primarily funded the CCA. This new law likely would or certainly could create a boom in treason prosecutions, make it virtually impossible for released or

paroled felons to re-integrate into society, and set the stage for the United States of America to become the most heavily incarcerated country in the history of the world.

2. Moreover, Senator Goofball would have pointed out, to the extent that one could blame 831 on convicted felons, more often than not those convicted felons consisted of ex-military fighters who, upon coming back from their tours of duty, found themselves with raging cases of PTSD, no jobs, no benefits, inadequate care, and not much else to do but let their PTSD lead them into the imprudent acts that led them to prison in the first place.

To be fair, some people would have debated that. The military had long possessed drones that could be launched from anywhere in the world, with no boots on the ground. But when the wrong drone got launched and hit the country of Georgia in 2025, America radically changed its policy. The USA avoided a probable world war that it did not care to fight, and went back to the conventional Army, Navy, Air Force and Marines way of controlling the world. By 2049 some factions of the military and Congress thought the blowback from the Georgia incident had run its course, and business could carry on as usual. Others thought it would never go away, and shouldn't.

But no speech and debate happened. O'Keefe and Radley ramrodded the Super Patriot Act of 2049 through Congress, with the support of the Attorney General, and it became law by October 1, 2049.

And then, the policy wonks at the Department of Justice ("DOJ") went to work and proceeded to define the term 'enemy of the State' in the Code of Federal Regulations ("CFR's").

Under the official definition, an 'enemy of the State' consisted of someone who was sentenced to a term of prison and had served time in the penitentiary, state or federal, or had committed a felony offense that was *punishable* by a mandatory minimum term of imprisonment, anywhere in the country.

In other words, if hypothetically one committed a crime whereby s/he didn't go to prison, but in some other jurisdiction (federal or state) for the same conduct s/he would have mandatorily gone to prison for a minimum term of imprisonment, s/he was an "enemy of the State." That meant Adam Kolkoski was by definition an "enemy of the State," since for his offense he would have been sentenced to prison for at least five years in the federal system, even if not in the state system where he had been granted probation.

Horrified, the ACLU took this law up immediately to the Supreme Court of the United States on a constitutional challenge. But in a 5-4 vote, the SCOTUS held that the law was not unconstitutional. The high Court also held that under this law, one did not have to *know* he was harboring an "enemy of the State." He only had to intend to harbor someone who *happened to be* an "enemy of the State."

Critics reacted strongly. Some called it the most politically expedient, wrongly decided SCOTUS case in the paranoid atmosphere of perceived insurrection since the Japanese internment camp decision post-Pearl Harbor in *Korematsu v. United States*. They argued that this opinion in time would ensure a boom in incarceration that only would increase the taxpayers' burden to the CCA. It didn't help matters that the swing vote on the SCOTUS had been the former general counsel for the Corrections Corporation of America, yet he didn't see a need to recuse himself.

But it didn't matter. By January of 2051, the body politic of the United States of America was stuck with the "Super Patriot Act of 2049." And Pastor Beau Browne had unknowingly, but nevertheless unlawfully, agreed to harbor "an enemy of the State" in Adam Kolkoski.

IV

In one of the last decisions of the Roberts Court before John Roberts left the Supreme Court after 35 years as the Chief Justice, the Supreme Court of the United States granted certiorari on a case regarding the issue of torture. The Court decided that when an individual residing in the US is suspected of acts of treason against the US and the Executive Branch hadn't decided whether to proceed militarily or in criminal courts, the FBI could lawfully engage in acts of torture in its interrogation of such suspects and use their statements against them. Prior to the Super Patriot Act of 2049, this decision generated some controversy; some people in the US still felt bothered by the prospect of "torturing folks." But the decision didn't have quite the controversy it could have had otherwise, as the tortured individual involved in the case consisted of a second-generation ISIS who had resided illegally in the United States. But it remained the law in the wake of the passage of the Super Patriot Act of 2049.

As a result of the state registration laws, Adam Kolkoski had to report that his new address consisted of the parsonage of the Congregational Church within 48 hours of the move. The local sheriff did some crosschecking, and reported this fact to the FBI. On January 23, 2051, two agents from the FBI paid a visit to Beau Browne.

But these weren't just any two agents. These two G-men, Special Agents Dombrowski and Gluck, came advertised and known throughout the agency and the community by their nicknames of "Agent Doom" and "Agent Gloom." These two, along with Special Agent Borland, aka "Agent Boom" –- although "Boom" wasn't needed for this particular job – formed part of an elite sub agency: The Special Investigation Squad for Terrorist Elimination & Retribution. The acronym: "SISTER." Gloom, Doom and (sometimes) Boom collectively wore the moniker of "The Sister Act."

Beau went to answer the door. His wife was at a Thursday Night Congregational Ladies Club gathering at the church. But he never had the chance to open the door. The local SWAT police smashed down his parsonage door with an Army tank. In the "shock and awe" mode, Gloom and Doom jumped out of the tank holding M-16A10's – advanced weaponry that could on every shot knock the eyes out of a gnat from 1,000 yards away - and wearing paramilitary outfits and protective helmets.

"Can I help you?" asked a trembling Beau.

They showed Pastor Browne their badges. "Where's Kolkoski?"

Beau, taken aback, said "Who?"

"Don't give me that!" Snarled Doom, smacking Pastor Browne on the back of his knee with his M-16A10. "You know who Kolkoski is! Where is he?"

"Probably cleaning the church's ladies room. Why? Did he do something wrong?"

"No, you did!" replied Gloom.

"What are you talking about?" Beau experienced a wave of intense fear.

Gloom commenced the interrogation. "Kolkoski lives here, doesn't he?"

"Well, yes, temporarily, until he can get on his feet."

"What do you mean, 'temporarily'?"

"Well," gulped Beau, "he told me he was down on his luck because of the Adam Walsh Law and couldn't find a home or a job. I agreed to take him in for the time being and give him a job as a janitor at the church until he could get back on his feet."

"What else did he tell you?" Gloom interrogated.

"Well, that he was a convicted sex offender because a jury didn't believe his claim about being entrapped by the police 45 years ago on the Internet."

"Did he tell you his sentence?"

"Yes. He said he was given probation in state court, and completed all of his sex therapy classes and was honorably discharged from probation. He says he has never been in trouble with the law again since then."

"Did you check his background? Did you check his story?"

"Well, no, but he's been a parishioner here for years. I've never known him to lie, or to be less than honorable."

Then Gloom delivered the bad news to Pastor Browne: "Did you know that if Kolkoski had been prosecuted for that in federal court, he would have gone to prison for at least five years?"

Browne looked at Gloom, aghast. "You're not serious, are you?"

Doom moved forward and smacked the Pastor in the mouth with the butt of his rifle. "Do we look like we are making this up?"

Beau now started to feel even more intense fear. "Why did you do that?"

"Because you have harbored an enemy of the State," intoned Gloom.

Without thinking, Browne again said, "What? You really believe I did this?"

After the second rifle smack in the mouth, which drew blood, Browne sunk to his knees, looked up at the SISTER Act, and asked, "Why did you do that?"

"Because you have violated the Super Patriot Act of 2049."

"What? I couldn't have! – No!..."

But this time Beau got three smacks in the mouth.

"Why are you doing this to me?"

"Because you are a terrorist!"

Beau spit out blood. "Terrorist? This is insane? I'm not.... Don't..."

At this point Doom threw Beau to the ground. Gloom stomped and kicked him. Beau cried out: "Stop! I want a lawyer!"

Doom mocked him like a 10-year-old: "I want a lawyer! I want a lawyer!" And then in his normal, shrill tone of voice, he sneered, "Well, you don't get a lawyer! John Roberts said so!"

"Who's John Roberts?"

Gloom got a gleam in his eyes. "Who's John Roberts...?" Then he tased Beau and, for good measure, ground his boot in the back of Beau's head. "You want to be a smart ass, don't you?"

At this point Beau was sobbing. "Stop! Stop! What do you want from me?"

"We want your confession! You were plotting to overthrow the federal government, weren't you?"

"No!!"

Gloom grabbed Beau by the little bit of hair Beau had left and screamed in his face: "You're lying! We know you're lying! You couldn't pass a polygraph right now! You'd be so far off the chart on the flunk scale that you'd embarrass yourself! We know! This is what we do for a living! We've been doing this long enough! We know! We know a liar when we see one! You're a liar!"

"I'm not lying!"

Gloom kicked Pastor Browne in the head, and when Beau twitched involuntarily, Gloom tased him. At that point Beau lay on the ground of his home, his castle, motionless. Doom bent down, and could tell Beau was still breathing from the heaviness of his breath.

"It's the old 'possum act,' Gloom. He thinks we're so dumb. Let's take him to the 'Baptismal Tank' for a little more interrogation!"

And the SISTER Act handcuffed Beau and dragged him off to FBI headquarters, to the "Terrorist Baptismal Tank" for a little bit of "confessional."

As soon as Beau saw the tank, he knew what he faced and started to scream. "No!!"

"So, you want to scream like a little baby boy, do you?" Sneered Doom. The two law enforcement officers slugged Beau in his solar plexus, so as to disable him. Gloom and Doom then strapped Pastor Browne on to the board. "We'll give you one more chance, Browne! Do you intend to overthrow the US Government?"

At this point, Pastor Browne knew that there were two things not to say: "No!" and "Are you serious?" But what could he do? Lie, capitulate and say, "Yes?" That would probably result in a beating that would take his life.

So, Pastor Browne said this: "Blessed are the poor in spirit, for theirs will be the Kingdom of Heaven."

"Ah, a wise guy, eh?" Gloom tipped the board over, and Beau went into the tank for about 10 seconds. When they brought him back to the air, Doom said, "What were you saying? Do you want to start over?"

Pastor Browne continued: "Blessed are those who mourn, for they will be comforted."

"Yep, a wise guy, all right," sneered Gloom. And this time Beau went into the tank for another 12 seconds. They brought him back to the air, and Doom sneered, "And what else do you want to say, Reverend Do-gooder?"

"Blessed are the meek, for they shall inherit the earth."

"Oh, so now you want to leave a last will and testament? That's a pretty good idea, Browne!" And Beau went into the tank for another 13 seconds. They brought him back up. Beau gasped for air even more loudly. Doom sneered even louder, as he got right into Pastor Browne's face. "We can't *hear* you! We can't *hear you*!! What else you got to say?"

"Blessed are those who hunger and thirst for righteousness, for they will be filled."

"Yeah, you are self-righteous, we'll give you that!" Dunk, down another 14, up. "Ready to confess yet, Browne?"

Beau gagged, and was barely able to spit out, "Blessed are the merciful, for they will be shown mercy."

"And blessed are the wise, for they will be shown wisdom!" laughed Doom. And down went Pastor Browne for another 11. When they brought him up, Doom asked, "Ready to confess now, Browne?"

"Blessed are the pure in heart, for they will see God."

"So, you want to see God, do you?" Sneered Gloom. This time, the 12 seconds felt longer. When Beau came up he was starting to turn blue. "Ready yet? Answer me! Answer me! Ready yet?"

By this time, Beau had urinated in the cold water, his lips quivered, and he choked back tears. "Blessed are the peacemakers, for they will be called children of God."

Doom laughed. "Yeah, you're going to need a pacemaker pretty soon! Ready to confess now, Browne?" And down into the yellow tank went Pastor Browne, this time for 15 seconds. By now, it felt like 15 minutes. When he came up gagging and three shades of blue, Doom said, "We are going to break you down, Browne. We will outlast you."

Beau was more stubborn than the SISTER Act had initially calculated. "Blessed are those who are persecuted because of righteousness, for theirs is the kingdom of heaven." And one more 15-second dunk. When Beau came up, he breathed so loudly and rapidly he could barely speak.

Gluck said, "All right, I think that's enough for today. No, wait. Let's put him in a pig sty and make him run on all fours and squeal like one!"

Dombrowski glowered at Gluck. "Don't you ever read the FBI Interrogation Manual, Gluck? We only do that to the fucking Arabs!"

And it all didn't matter, anyway. The FBI had their confession. They didn't have their "super confession"; but it didn't matter. With or without the baptismal waterboarding, they had their "slam dunk" case. They arrested Pastor Beau Browne and drove him to jail, where they charged him with treason, by reason of violating the Super Patriot Act of 2049.

V

"Look at you! Look at that belly! Here I spend all this money on a state-of-the-art home gym, and you let yourself become a fat pig like this! What's the matter with you?"

Bonita Browne's flash of anger and resentment, upon hearing those words, turned inward to its usual position of shame. Once again, she said nothing to her spouse and turned away.

Since 2015 the years hadn't gone quite so smoothly for Bonita Browne, Beau's younger sister. Bonita was gay, and had been trapped in a long-time lesbian relationship with her lover, Esperanza Lopez. Some marriages may be made in heaven; this one was not.

They married when Bonita was 20-years-old. Bonita was nervous about breaking the news to Tania, her Christian fundamentalist mother. Predictably, when she did, Tania lost her composure.

"You are marrying a woman? What is the matter with you? Marriage is between a man and a woman only!"

Bonita had always found it difficult to confront her mother. "Where in the Bible does it say that, Mommy?"

"Leviticus 18 and 20. Read your Bible!"

Bonita did not have a snappy response to that. So, she went to her older brother, Beau. He would know how to confront his mother on the subject. He always did.

"Mother, what about Romans 13 and Galatians 8?"

"*Hijo mio*, you are arguing with me again. If Bonita marries that woman, she is disinherited. Don't make me disinherit you, too!"

But Bonita, stubborn as she was underneath her sunny and mild surface, disobeyed her mother and married Esperanza. When that happened, Tania indeed disinherited Bonita. And when that happened, Beau and their father, Ryan, Tania's ex-husband, arranged to have Bonita inherit Ryan's entire estate, so that both Beau and Bonita would inherit. Ryan trusted his children to make it even between them after he and Tania passed, and they did.

The marriage had its problems from the beginning, however.

Although they were only a few years apart in age, Esperanza had a case of endometriosis that prevented her from being able to conceive. The two wanted to have a child, however. Thus, Esperanza fertilized Bonita with cryogenically frozen sperm from a sperm bank, using a turkey baster. Bonita gave birth to Antonio Lopez-Browne. Bonita hoped for another child. Esperanza drew the line at one. Antonio was an only child.

As a toddler, Antonio first referenced his parents as "Momma Bo" and "Momma Panz." But as he grew older, Antonio adjusted to Bonita as "Momma" and to Esperanza as "Mother." Antonio also adjusted to a household that perpetually had varying degrees of turbulence inside of its walls.

Bonita stayed home and raised Antonio, while Esperanza worked long hours as a very high-powered civil litigator. She specialized in construction defect litigation, and she made millions – defiantly proving her worth to her family, who thought she would forever remain poor, and had wasted good student loan money on law school.

But Esperanza became a self-made millionaire by being a "scorched earth," uncivil, high-pressured lawyer. But for the sexual difference, some might have called her an "alpha male." Some did, anyway. And the more that people called her a "bitch" behind her back, the more she thrived on intimidating whomever she needed to intimidate to get her way.

Esperanza simply didn't care what people thought of her, or so it seemed. By all appearances, all that mattered to her was to win. After all, she had three strikes against her: She was a woman, she was gay, and she was Hispanic. Meaning, to make it in the world of construction defect litigation, she had to scorch a lot of earth. And so she did. She won, early and often.

Esperanza also consistently filed bar and judicial complaints against a record number of lawyers and judges who got in her way. The fact that the state bar and the state judicial discipline commission got to the point where they practically threw the complaints into the nearest trash can as soon as they saw her signature to them didn't matter. Those lawyers and judges who didn't agree with her opinions would have hell to pay.

And she brought that personality home, as she verbally humiliated Bonita and Antonio, but primarily Bonita, on a constant basis.

"Momma," said the eight-year-old Antonio one day, "How did you get those bruises on your nose and cheek?"

Bonita at first said nothing, and then looking at the ground, said, "I tripped and fell while walking in the garden."

"What did you trip on?"

Bonita did not want to talk about it, and mumbled something.

"I'm sorry, Momma. What did you say?"

"Some tree roots that came up from the grass."

"And you didn't throw your hands out to break your fall?" The perceptive pre-teenager asked.

"No. Not in time."

Antonio was able to tell from the age of eight that Bonita's excuses were lies. But he was a sensitive, withdrawn boy. Not being like anyone else in school, Antonio attracted bullies constantly. Antonio had enough problems of his own, and never wanted to confront either woman about his mother's treatment of his momma.

Bonita, in turn, wanted to leave the subject of her wife's tongue-lashings of her son alone. Bonita did her best to "explain" Antonio's mother to the boy over the years. They both wanted to believe the excuses.

Why did Bonita put up with the abuse? It took Antonio years of talking with Bonita and analyzing the situation, but he finally figured it out. In the early years, Bonita's abiding goal was to spite her mother. She refused to allow the words "I told you so!" to emanate from Tania's lips. As she grew older, however, and once Tania had passed, Bonita's motives became more mixed and unclear.

For one thing, although gay marriage had long been legalized and federally enforced by that time, institutions still maintained a rather derisive and disbelieving attitude toward a gay woman who claimed to be in an "abusive" gay relationship. Battered women's shelters were for straight women, battered by brutish men. Even then, society had a difficult time believing that a woman could or would systematically abuse another woman, despite any and all evidence to the contrary. Bonita experienced that form of discrimination and segregation on a constant basis. She felt like a second-class citizen because she was one. Bonita never could visualize first-class.

For another, the Lopez-Browne household had money, and the two women lived a lavish lifestyle. They owned a 5,000 square foot home on a heavily wooded two-acre lot, with an in-ground swimming pool and hot tub, home movie theatre, tennis court and an outdoor sauna. Esperanza bleached her hair blonde and stayed thin and youngish-looking due to an obsessive amount of tennis, swimming, treadmill running, spa treatments and plastic surgery. She also owned a second-to-none wardrobe of designer dresses. Both women displayed high visibility on the society pages of a number of on-line newspapers and magazines. Bonita and Esperanza took fancy Caribbean cruises together, although generally the two women stayed in separate cabins. Esperanza also owned a private art collection with original Renoir's, Van Gogh's, and Wyeth's (Andrew, of course, but certainly not Jamie) that also topped the line. Bonita felt that she couldn't change the status quo. More that that, she felt she wasn't entitled to change the status quo. Basically, Bonita Browne smiled tightly in public and suffered silently in private, appreciating albeit not enjoying the money.

Instead, Bonita found her life's affirmance in her church and in her son. She stayed in the marriage, determined to have Antonio experience as "normal" an upbringing as possible. And as the years rolled on, Bonita and Antonio's connection became tighter, while Bonita's appearance became plainer and her waistline grew wider.

As a young woman Bonita was even more beautiful than her Costa Rican mother; Bonita initially was "eye candy" on the arm of Esperanza. Esperanza not only knew it, but also reveled in it. But as the years of abuse wore her down, Bonita's quirks in Esperanza's eyes transformed from charmingly endearing to royally annoying. Anyone studying Bonita could see her withdrawn body language, her tightly tied-back hair, her bowed head and lack of eye contact, and the redness in her fingertips from digging one set of fingernails into the other fingers – and with careful enough perusal, her occasional bruises.

Bonita's only reminder of her one-time beauty came in the form of young Antonio, who certainly inherited his momma's beautiful chin, lips, nose and eyes (along with the sperm donor's rock-star hair and statuesque stance). But for his part, Antonio dealt with the domestic atmosphere by becoming a superstar. As a young man, he felt extraordinarily driven to succeed and to overcome the constant abuse at the hands and mouth of his mother. The older he grew, the more averse he grew to his mother's opinions.

As one example, once when he was in college and studying art history, Antonio made the mistake of suggesting to Esperanza that Jackson Pollock had a larger impact on 20th century art than Andrew Wyeth.

"Oh, that's ridiculous!" Snorted Esperanza, again bullying her son into submission. "Art professors! Just a bunch of 'know-nothings' who aren't capable of doing anything but 'teaching the uninformed!'"

"Mother," responded Antonio. "The Professor says that an original Pollock hanging in the Bellagio Gallery should fetch three times what an Andrew Wyeth would fetch."

"Pollock! Bah! He was nothing more than a 'glorified finger-painter'! Anyone who pays more than a dime for a Pollock is an idiot!"

Antonio swallowed his hurt, and simply studied the situation harder, so that if the subject ever came up again he would state the definitive case for Pollock with more bravado. He would become a "Pollock expert". Until that time, or other like times, Antonio did his best to hibernate in his room, study, and become "the expert" on everything that his mother merely pretended to be.

By all rights, young girls should have flocked to a gorgeous young man like Antonio. But Antonio, albeit not gay, felt that he could not send out signals of interest to any beautiful young lady, for fear of some kind of harsh opinionated correction from his mother. Whatever the correction would be, Antonio grew to the point of refusing to listen to it. So, Antonio stayed in his room, and channeled his sexual frustrations into his studies.

And there, Antonio studied with single-minded, intense obsession. Antonio did not have friends at school or in the neighborhood; who could have empathy for a boy like this? Who could possibly walk a mile in this lad's shoes? After all, at ages 13-18 brainiacs are to be envied, not admired, especially rich young brainiacs. And that would be even truer of rich young brainiac sons of two gay women. Antonio's only friend was his Uncle Beau.

So, Antonio graduated from high school with a perfect 1600 on the SAT; obtained a scholarship from Stanford; graduated magna cum laude in economics; and went to law school at Columbia. There, he achieved the position of editor of the Columbia Law Review, before he graduated in 2047.

With a background like that, Antonio had punched his ticket for life. He could have followed in Esperanza's footsteps if he had wanted to. But he didn't want to. Fueled by his long talks with the biggest influence on his life, his Uncle Beau, Antonio had graduated with a high level of idealism. Upon graduating from Columbia, Antonio went to work for the National Legal Aid Foundation for about three years. He felt a duty to the legal system to help the downtrodden. And in America by 2049, an awful lot of downtrodden people who needed help lurked everywhere.

But by 2050, even Antonio had burned out. That job caused burnout to anyone who held it. The job consisted of 60 hours per week of representing a never-ending sea of bipolars, schizophrenics, ADHD'ed and chronically depressed people. That description defined a huge percentage of America's populace by that time. All of that would try the resolve of any reasonable person. But Antonio found it even more difficult to deal with the law. By that time the law had set the poor up almost always to lose.

     Fighting one losing eviction battle and losing car repossession after another proved to be too much for young Antonio's ego and feeling of self-worth. In January of 2051 Antonio hung out his shingle and started his own law practice.

VI

Antonio promptly went to the jail, the first person to visit Pastor Browne. "Uncle Beau, what happened?"

Beau did his best to relive and retell his night of terror at the hands of the SISTER Act. At times he hesitated and hyperventilated, while his face turned red. He spoke in halting, clipped phrases. But Antonio, young and inexperienced, assumed that his uncle was showing emotional difficulties. Antonio felt swept away by the emotion of the moment.

Above all, Antonio experienced horror. As he reacted like the bright, idealistic young lawyer that he was, he thought, *what gives the FBI the right to think they can drive an army tank into the front door of a Congregational pastor's parsonage? And then torture a man of the cloth like this? And mock the Sermon on the Mount in the process? Who the hell do they think they are? They must know that a Congregational pastor cannot be a terrorist! This can't be right! This has to be a human rights violation!*

As Antonio left the jail and thought about what he had just witnessed and heard, he alighted on two thoughts: First, he had to find a lawyer for his uncle who would stand up to the US government; and second, he had to find somebody in the media who could wake America up to the unjust state of the union that the United States had become. He had in mind the identity of that attorney; but he also had in mind that the attorney more likely would take the case if she knew that the public was on Uncle Beau's side.

At that point in time *Mother Jones* magazine barely operated on a shoestring as an Internet magazine only. But Antonio figured that if he could find an enterprising, idealistic young journalist to cover the story, maybe that journalist could find a way to publicize the story through social media. And such a young journalist likely would work for or at *Mother Jones*.

So, Antonio found such a young, idealistic reporter, a former campus rabble-rouser whom Antonio vaguely knew at Stanford. The reporter had become an independent journalist who broke stories to *Mother Jones* and others. She also felt horror from Antonio's story. The young journalist checked the court filings, talked to Beau, Antonio and Beau's wife, didn't talk to the SISTER Act (who wouldn't have talked to some young skank from *Mother Jones* in any event), and broke the story.

Before long, every progressive news organization in the country ran the Beau Browne story nationwide on Facebook memes. By 2051, Facebook had merged with Linked-In, Tumbler, Twitter, Instagram, Pinterest, Google-Plus, and every other form of social media that had existed or had popped up since 2015. Almost everyone communicated by Facebook, whether they cared for social media or not. The memes received over a million hits a day. Plenty of people had a strong, negative reaction to what the FBI had done to Pastor Browne.

And all of this ultimately came to the attention of Deacon Joe Green.

Joseph D'Anthony Green, a former tent preacher turned Second Baptist Church Deacon from Chicago, enjoyed the enduring reputation as a social activist, and a charismatic, dynamic speaker who could instantly connect with most anybody. He epitomized the closest thing anybody had seen to

Martin Luther King, Jr. since Martin Luther King, Jr. because, much like Christ Himself, they didn't seem to care about political causes directly. Deacon Joe Green would never run for President of the United States or for Congress, or appear as a talking head on Fox News, CNN or MSNBC. Deacon Joe Green knew he could wield more influence on the body politic from the perspective of the pulpit. True, nobody marched on Washington in his name; but by 2051 nobody marched on Washington for any reason.

More importantly, Deacon Joe Green had never been caught up in either a sex or a money scandal, although the FBI tried desperately to find one. But Deacon Joe Green had plenty of handlers around him who did their jobs well in keeping him away from curious journalists, paparazzi, and the FBI, and vice versa.

Deacon Joe Green also was the owner of "The Calvary Jamboree" Park, a series of Christian-themed amusement parks that had arisen all over the country. And he owned the rights to a Sunday morning program, streamed into millions of tablets and simulcast in Baptist churches throughout America. Deacon Joe Green enjoyed more popularity and reverence in 2051 than Jesse Jackson, Al Sharpton, Pat Robertson, Jimmy Swaggart or Jim Bakker had ever experienced. The nation longed for a "rock-star from the pulpit", and Deacon Joe Green filled the need.

And on a Sunday morning in early March of 2051, the nation heard the words of Deacon Joe Green:

"Brothers and sisters! Did not Jesus, yes, *Jesus Himself*, tell us all to love thy neighbor as you would yourself? Did He not say that? *Yes* – He not only said it and historians told us about it in the Gospel of Mark and the Gospel of Matthew, Jesus said it was the greatest Commandment of all! Of *all*!! Love thy neighbor as *thyself*! The whole idea was in Leviticus, even before Jesus Christ was *alive*! The foundation of *Christianity*! For that matter, the foundation of *religion*! *Any religion!* Love thy neighbor as thyself! For when you do that, you love *God*! And when you love God, you are on your way to the kingdom of *heaven*!

And now we turn to what is happening out west of here. Brother Beau Browne, the pastor of a Congregational Church, loved his neighbor. He *loved* a man who was down on his luck. A man who had been unfairly persecuted by the police. That's right. The *police*! For 45 years! *45 years*!! A man unfairly persecuted by the police for *45 years*!!

Brother Browne *loved* this man! Took him into his *home*! Just like we do at the Calvary Jamboree! Gave him *food*! Gave him *shelter*! Gave him a *job*! Gave him *comfort*! Gave him the self-respect he hadn't had for years! *For years*! Just like we do, over and over, at the Calvary Jamboree!

And for that, what happened? The FBI said Brother Browne committed treason! *Treason*!! They despised him! They tortured him! That's right, they *tortured* a Christian preacher! They invaded his home with an army tank! An *army tank*! 'Shock and awe' to a gentle Congregational preacher? A man's home is his castle, except when it's a parsonage? Well, why not? The United States government has to win a war *some* time! It's been too *long* for them!

And when Brother Browne preached the Sermon on the Mount to these Godless thugs, what did the FBI do? They tortured him some *more*! And I'll bet they *enjoyed* it, too! Just like the Godless thugs that they *are*! Our FBI employs Godless *thugs*! If you are a Godless thug, then *hurry, hurry*, step right *up*! There is a career in law enforcement, just waiting for *you* at the *FBI*!

Now, why do I say Godless? Do they not know or remember what Jesus Christ preached? Have they forgotten what Jesus Christ stands for? Take *care* of your neighbor when he is *hurt*! *Bandage his wounds*! Do they not remember the parable of the Good Samaritan? Do they not remember what Jesus taught us? Take him into your *Inn*! Well, that's what Brother Browne did! Just like what we do at the Calvary Jamboree – *every day*! And for that they tortured Brother Browne! They *despised* him!

This country *claims* to be based on Christian principles. But I say to *you*, brothers and sisters, when American government thinks it's the *Christian* thing to do to *torture* someone like Brother Browne who has loved his *neighbor*, who has been the good *Samaritan*, what do I say to American government? I don't say God bless America! I say God *curse* America! That's *right*! *God curse* America! But I am not cussing like a schoolboy on the schoolyard! I'm not telling you this only so that certain *elements* of the *media* can *pretend* to be *indignant* at my *message*!

Brothers and sisters, I tell you this: God will *condemn* America for letting its laws come to this! How can we *do* this to ourselves and call ourselves a *Christian nation*? What is the *matter* with us? What has led us to *think* this way? Do the lawmakers and the police need to spend a week at the Calvary Jamboree in order to come to their *senses*?

What innocent, God-fearing man or woman will be the *next victim* of the Terrorist Baptismal Tank? And I ask you, brothers and sisters, what does *waterboarding* have to do with *baptism*, anyway? John the Baptist meant baptism for cleansing of *sins*! But the FBI isn't interested in *that!* The FB*I* means baptism for *punishment*! That's not cleansing of sins! That's cleansing of *goodness*, cleansing of *righteousness*, cleansing of *mercy*!

How did America let itself become a nation that cleanses *goodness*? Why is our government against *goodness*? The song

'America the Beautiful' speaks of our heroes, who loved mercy more than life! But I say to you, we have become nothing but a nation of *cowards*, wrapped in the clothing of *bullies*, who *despise mercy*! We do not live in a nation of *heroes*! We live in a nation of *cowards*!

I tell you, we *fool* ourselves into believing we're the *greatest* nation on *earth*! How can a nation that cleanses goodness from our souls, or tries to, like the FBI tried to do to Brother Browne, *delude* itself into thinking it's the greatest nation on earth? I repeat, brothers and sisters, and journalists, write this down: *God curse America*!!"

Across the nation the sermon riveted America. Unfortunately, Judge Edwin Charles Norcross, the United States District Judge who had been assigned the case of <u>United States of America v. Beau Ezekiel Browne</u>, included himself in the list of "rivetees." The following Monday he wrote an Order without a pending motion, that said the following:

"Yesterday, I listened to the sermon of Deacon Joe Green, as he talked about the above-captioned case to which I have been assigned. I replayed it and listened to it a second time. And then a third. And as I thought about the sermon I realized: I cannot be a fair jurist in this case. To the Government, that is. Everyone who comes to court deserves a fair trial, and that includes the Government. When I cannot be fair to the Government, it is time to recuse myself. And thus I do. I order the Chief Judge of this District to reassign this cause to a Judge who will give both sides a fair trial."

In the law, there exists "the law of unintended consequences." Whatever Deacon Joe Green may have intended by his sermon, he could not have intended what happened next. The Chief Judge did indeed reassign the case – to the Honorable Jonah Hixson, Senior United States District Judge.

Jonah Hixson was a tall, thin man who seemed to have a perpetual scowl on his face, a scowl so deep that his look almost came from behind himself. Hixson had enjoyed his reputation as a young career prosecutor, a law-and-order conservative, and a bagman for the GOP when President George W. Bush put him on the bench, some 45 years ago. At that time the legal community regarded Hixson as a legal wunderkind at the age of 40. His more contemporary critics – of which there were many – contended that Hixson should have completely retired at least ten years ago. Ever since the tragic death of his wife in 2031 and the refusal of President Rubio to elevate him to the court of appeals, Hixson had become even more surly and even more single-minded and hardheaded than anyone had ever seen. He became the kind of judge about whom the lawyers and litigants could predict only one thing: By trial's end, he would strive to and succeed in royally and unjustifiably upsetting somebody. In criminal cases, that status usually belonged to the defendant and/or his lawyer. In civil cases, the list of angry people included anybody, sometimes everybody. The national book on bad federal judges had him toward the top. Since 2031 Hixson had not asked a single legal question of any lawyer from the bench. He didn't have to. Nothing that any fool lawyer could tell him could make him change his mind on anything.

Perhaps even worse, he had never lost his zeal as a prosecutor. As a young Department of Justice lawyer, Hixson proudly displayed his motto on his office wall: "If it moves, prosecute it!" He held the motto more strongly as the years rolled on. Over time, Hixson had been named that state's "Prosecutor of the Year" for nine years – as a federal judge. He gladly accepted the award each time, oblivious to the irony of a judge being named "Prosecutor of the Year."

By all rights, Hixson should have been the most reversed district court judge in the circuit. But over the years the new judges the various Presidents had put on the Circuit Court of Appeals were almost as hardheaded, single-minded, and pro-government as Hixson. And by all appearances, that gave Hixson that much more courage to try to set the all-time record for the most harmless errors committed in a single trial. On one case he got up to six. Six demonstrable mistakes during a five-day jury trial. But not enough mistakes to tip over the judgment of some first-time tax cheat whom Hixson hit with a sentence of 180 months imprisonment.

  In short, things looked really, really bad for Brother Beau Browne.

VII

Antonio continued to visit his Uncle Beau in jail. Beau had been appointed a perfectly competent attorney. But Antonio could see that, with the reputation of Hixson, "perfect competence" wasn't going to be enough for his Uncle Beau.

As Antonio saw it, Uncle Beau needed a lawyer with the ruthless character to get in the DOJ lawyer's and Hixson's combined face. That lawyer also would have to prove smart enough to figure out where the weaknesses in the Government's case lay. And that lawyer would have to prove idealistic enough and charismatic enough to instill energy into those that mattered. The injustice of Uncle Beau's case would have to capture their imaginations and sweep them away.

In short, Pastor Browne needed a dream team for this case. But a dream team on a Congregational pastor's income didn't seem too probable. So, Uncle Beau would have to prioritize. And under the circumstances, the lawyer would have to be, first and foremost, a meanie. A fire ant in scorpion's clothing.

"Please, Mother, would you represent Uncle Beau? Please?"

Esperanza gave her son the stink-eye. "Come on, Antonio. You know I don't practice criminal law. Besides, the court gave your uncle a perfectly competent lawyer. That's good enough."

"No, it is not, Mother. Judge Hixson will humiliate that lawyer into submission, and make sure that jury convicts Uncle Beau. We have to do something for Uncle Beau."

Esperanza looked at her son and snapped. "The last time I did something for a Browne, I advanced $10,000 to your grandfather so he could hire that private investigator, the famous Jessie Parker. And I didn't get repaid for a year – and no interest besides."

Bonita piped in. "Yes, and my father was in jail for most of that year, and he paid you back pretty shortly after he was released."

"Shut up," snapped Esperanza again. "This doesn't concern you." Bonita put her head down and again did what she was told.

Esperanza then turned to her son: "But I'm sure you think I'm going to represent your uncle for free. No, no, no! I'm running a business here, not a legal aid clinic!"

Bonita responded, "I'll pay your fee out of my inheritance. Just help my brother, please."

Before Esperanza could say "Are you deaf? Deaf? Did I say 'gosh, I don't know?' or did I say 'No!'" like she always did, Antonio jumped into the conversation:

"Mother, look, I know you don't practice criminal law. But this is the most famous case in America right now! Look, Uncle Beau has no less than Deacon Joe Green of Chicago on his side! How often do you get a chance to handle a criminal case like this, where you're representing the good guy? And with Deacon Joe Green cheering you on? Don't you want to be involved with the most famous case in America? Don't you want to be a hero?"

"Not when I am unaware of the first thing about criminal law!"

"But you do know the first thing about trying a case. And you do know how to handle bullies who get in your way!"

Esperanza paused. Antonio thought he could read her mind: She had made her money. She had made her mark on the civil litigation world. Still, to handle the most famous case in America – and where she did not represent some rapist, murderer or large-scale con artist…. The thought appeared to intrigue her….

Esperanza finally replied: "If I could get someone to associate with me, someone who could give me some pointers on how to handle a case like this and handle this judge, well, maybe…."

Antonio had been waiting for just that opening. "It just so happens I have somebody in mind."

"You do? Whom do you know after a few years of representing poor people on evictions and repossessions that could jump into a case like this?"

"Nobody personally. But Professor Carter was my supervisor on the law review at Columbia. And he used to talk a lot about his good friend at Cornell, Professor Dockett!"

That stopped Esperanza in her tracks. Most everybody including Esperanza, and not just criminal lawyers, had heard of Fred Dockett. Dockett wrote and edited the definitive treatise on criminal defense in federal court. Dockett also had a nickname known throughout the legal community as "Rocket Dockett." Or perhaps primarily prosecutors called Dockett that. Dockett taught trial practice as an adjunct professor at Cornell Law School. He was a throwback to Clarence Darrow of the 1920's and to the philosophies of the Warren Court of the 1950's and 1960's, though by 2051 very few people knew whom those people were. When Dockett decided to come on board on a case, he meticulously found a way to win and regularly did so.

Dockett also enjoyed his status on the legal talk show circuit, generally cutting any prosecutor to the quick without missing a beat. He had a mix of professorial, sartorial splendor and street-wise cynicism about him, spoken at the speed of sound bytes, which made him unique. Basically, Dockett could tell just about anyone with a high school education why some prosecutor was full of "nonsense" or "legal gibberish." And lawyers and non-lawyers alike imminently believed him – whether Dockett actually knew his subject matter or not.

Who wouldn't jump at the opportunity to work with someone like Fred Dockett?

Certainly, Antonio would. He added enthusiastically: "And if I can get Professor Dockett on board, I'll do the leg work. I'll do the research and do the investigation. I'll do what needs to be done. And Momma, you don't need to pay me; I'll talk to Auntie and see what she can do."

Esperanza paused for what seemed like an unnaturally long time, as both Antonio and Bonita stared at her. Finally, Esperanza said, "All right. As long as I'm lead counsel, and Dockett comes on board, I'm in."

Antonio hugged his mother. And Bonita said, "Thank you, Panz."

"Don't call me Panz!" shrieked Esperanza. "Don't ever call me Panz in front of Antonio again!"

Esperanza had never gone off on this particular issue before. Bonita appeared to add "Don't call her Panz in front of Antonio" to the already-lengthy "to-don't-do" list, dropped her head, looked at the ground, and walked away. Antonio walked with her. He put his arm around his momma's shoulder and pressed his head against hers in the all-too-familiar comfort position.

Esperanza simply thought: *Why do those two have to act like such pussies all of the time?*

Bail did not exist in the federal system for one charged with treason. And thus, Beau found himself locked up in the federal prisoner wing of the county jail. His cellie? None other than the infamous Simon Goldblatt.

Many people in the country had never heard of Simon Goldblatt. But most everybody knew something about Goldblatt's alias, Giovanni Ribaldi.

Ribaldi, a small, wiry man with a thick moustache and a loud, obnoxious laugh, distinguished himself as one with an incredible amount of energy. His metabolism appeared to be fueled by some kind of natural energy drink.

Beau eyed his cellmate suspiciously: "Aren't you the guy who ran for President of the United States in 2040?"

"Hah!" laughed the boisterous Ribaldi. "That's right! The nominee of the Sexual Liberation Party! 'One nation under Viagra!' When Merck threatened to sue me over that, I changed the campaign slogan to 'Stay the Inter-course!' I got 20.5% of the votes and 87.5% of the media attention!"

Beau continued that look toward Ribaldi. "Wasn't your candidacy just a PR stunt, like everyone claimed, to get people to watch 'The Artsy Fartsy' Show?"

"Hah! My piece de résistance! The 'Artsy Fartsy Show'! Young women, painting pictures in warehouses on easels with their boobs as artists' palates! Even younger woman playing

Jane with young men playing Tarzan, discovering sex in the jungle! Did you like that one where I had the bonobos cheering them on?"

"No, I never watched it."

"Never watched it? How could you miss it! Didn't you like the way I played the media to think young Tarzan and young Jane were going to have a threesome with the bonobo?"

Beau wrinkled his nose. "Disgusting. Why would you even do that?"

"It's showbiz, Baby! It's showbiz! Show me the money, Honey! And show me the money shot, while you're at it!" Ribaldi laughed that boisterous laugh and clapped Pastor Browne on the shoulder.

Pastor Browne felt willing to argue the premise. "Not showbiz when you hurt people. Girls that age don't know any better. And bestiality? Why do you corrupt those boys' and girls' morals?"

"Oh, nonsense!" Rejoined Ribaldi. "Haven't you been watching? You are so 20th Century in your beliefs! My girls do my show, and 10 years later they are A-list actresses in Hollywood! They never have to shoot a sex scene again if they don't want to! I give them their start! That's what they want!"

"That doesn't make it right," countered Browne.

"What are you talking about?" replied the manic Ribaldi. "Porn is everywhere, Baby! You can watch it on network television! Everywhere but the south – but they'll catch up! Those southerners start watching my show in 3-D, and they'll come around!"

Pastor Browne looked at Ribaldi. "I heard about the show where you had those girls making up lewd raps about Jesus and Mary Magdalene. That was disgusting!"

The jovial Ribaldi laughed. "Yeah, well, 79.5% of the people agreed with you! But 20.5% didn't! And millions of people bought the stream to that show to find out! How to run for President and make money! And all without a Super-Pac!"

"And what about the girl who 'played' Mary Magdalene?"

Ribaldi theatrically responded, "What about her? She went on 'American Idol III' after that and became a country and western superstar! She went to the media and renounced me! She said I made her do it! So I told the media the devil made her do it! Then she told them I was the devil! But I got her back: I gave a press conference and told everyone she was the spawn of the devil, and I had the birth certificate to prove it! Hah! Hah! hah! The media had a field day with that one! They actually hired forensic experts to examine the birth certificate and prove me wrong! And I claimed their so-called experts worked for Barack Obama! Hah! Hah! Hah! But she made her name for herself! She got what she wanted!"

Then Ribaldi whispered to Pastor Browne, "You see, there's something you don't understand about pornography!"

"What don't I understand that I want to know?"

Ribaldi laughed that laugh. "You're so funny! No, here's the secret: People are horny! They'll always be horny! Catholic priests? Still horny! Congregational Pastors like you? Incredibly horny! Rabbis? Oh, man, don't get me started! But people are sick and tired of 'I'm woman, you're man, let's fuck.' That format doesn't work any more! If porn were still underground, to where people always had to pay good money to watch it like in the good old days, then it would still work. You see. But now, with porn on television all the time, people see too much of it. They want it packaged differently. So, I give it to them! And they pay for it! Do I feel ashamed? Do you think I should feel ashamed? You want to know how I feel?"

Beau at this point wanted the conversation to end. "No."

"I'll tell you, anyway! I feel that any publicity is better than no publicity! It's Hollywood, Baby! It's all Hollywood! Why settle for 15 minutes of fame, when you can have 30? Whatever it takes to get people to pay good money to watch, that's all that matters!"

Pastor Browne tried to redirect the conversation. "What are you in for?"

Ribaldi laughed. "Luring a minor child into the production of pornography."

Beau rolled his eyes. "It figures."

Ribaldi responded, "No, I have a defense."

"What? You didn't do it?"

Giovanni snorted, "I didn't do it? What do you mean, 'I didn't do it'? Of course I did it! But what did I do? Some stupid production assistant misread the girl's birth certificate and thought she was 18 when I hired her to breast paint a picture on the sidewalk. She was 17 and 360 days. So, they say I'm looking at a mandatory minimum 20 years in prison. I missed freedom by five stinking days! Is that crazy? Is this law fucked up? I can fuck her brains out in my bedroom and be perfectly legal! But if I show her breast painting in a movie, I'm locked up for 20 years!"

"So your defense is the law is screwed up?"

Ribaldi continued with his show. "Well, from what I'm told, you should know something about that! But there is one difference between your case and mine."

"What?"

"I'm a political prisoner! The Government doesn't want me to run for President and steal votes from somebody ever again! That's why they're prosecuting me! Do they care about some 17-year-old whore? Of course not! Washington is persecuting me!"

"So how is that a defense again?" queried Pastor Browne.

"Did I say it was? I said I have a defense! I didn't tell you what it was! The whole world will find out, and when they do, I really will be President of the United States! 'Pathways to sexual freedom!' Let's not build a wall around the border! Let's build a giant peep-show booth! Right? Full employment for strippers in Brownsville, Nogales and National City! That will keep those damned Mexicans from wanting to come here! Take that, Donald Trump, you one-term has-been! There's your answer to illegal immigration! And that's just for starters!" And Ribaldi laughed that loud, obnoxious laugh.

It didn't take long for Beau Browne to notice some oddities beyond all that about Giovanni Ribaldi. Ribaldi could be heard during the evening barking out commands. No big deal *per se*; plenty of people in jail are schizoaffective, heard to bark out stream of consciousness *ad nauseum*. But Browne heard Ribaldi during the evening in their cell while Browne was out on the tier, barking out what sounded like orders to people sounding like assistants on what sounded like a cell phone. But inmates could not have cell phones. They could communicate with their lawyers by e-mail or jail videoconferencing during the day, but that was all of the allowable technology in jail. Where and how did Ribaldi get his cell phone?

Then there was the pizza box. Browne awakened one morning, and discovered that Ribaldi had eaten a pizza at midnight – and from the California Pizza Kitchen, not Dominos. Who was supplying Ribaldi with the free pizza? (And why wasn't he sharing?) (And what's with eating anchovies at midnight, anyway?) Ribaldi tore up the box into smaller pieces, so that it looked like part of his legal file and escaped the inspection of the "screws".

And on top of all of that, Ribaldi had a television set with a recording device set in the cell. No other inmate had a privilege like that. Ribaldi claimed he convinced the legal system that he needed to review the digitally captured evidence of the government, and his lawyers made special arrangements for the television and recorder. But most other pre-trial inmates had digitally captured evidence against them, yet didn't have television privileges like that. And Beau experienced enough interrupted sleep at night, from his upper bunk, with the sounds from the television, to know that Ribaldi really didn't care about the evidence against him to that extent. Somehow, Ribaldi had spliced and tapped into the cable plugged into the community dorm television, and thus diverted the signal to whatever he wanted to watch – including pay-per-view. He watched the type of evidence the government had against him for free, while other saps had to pay good money for the same pleasure.

One night Browne's curiosity got the better of him. He feigned sleep, and detected that Ribaldi had a visitor. Into the cell walked Michelle Dailey, the evening-shift matron.

It didn't take long for Browne to put it together. *That's how he gets the cell phone! Michelle Dailey brings it to him during the evening, leaves it in the cell, and takes it back at the end of her shift! And Ribaldi makes the calls from the cell, where the video cameras on the tier don't pick up what he is doing! Same thing with the pizza box and the television! And she probably deactivates the video camera in the unit for a few minutes when she comes on board her shift, so she doesn't get detected and can get away with it! But why?*

After that, Browne detected times when Michelle and Ribaldi would leave the cell for 15 minutes or so, before Ribaldi would quietly return without her. What were they up to? Did the jail have some mysterious room that the inmates didn't know about? Or did they traipse off to the "conjugal visit room," where they would go to have sex with each other?

Maybe so or maybe not, but Browne finally received some clues to the puzzle. One day a card fell out of Ribaldi's pulp fiction novel borrowed from the jail's library, a calling card. On the card's top the insignia read, "G & S Productions." And in the middle of the card with calligraphic first letters, the card read "Stephanie Stiletto."

Pastor Browne confronted Ribaldi. "Who is Stephanie Stiletto?"

Ribaldi looked down, looked up, looked around the room and said, "You're my minister, my priest, is that clear?"

"What do you mean?"

"I mean, everything I say to you and you say to me is privileged, because I am the penitent and you are the priest! Got it?"

Browne slowly responded, "Giovanni, you're not penitent about anything. But I get it. Whatever we say to each other is legally confidential. Right?"

"Right! So, here's the deal. She's going to get me out of here, if I don't win my trial. If I win my trial, we leave together. Either way, the 'Artsy Fartsy Show' has about run its course. And my new idea is to redo the old 'Ilsa: The She-Wolf of the S.S.' movie from 75 years ago, and star her as 'Stephanie Stiletto,' the new 'Ilsa.' My dear Michelle will be the new queen of mainstream BDSM!"

"And she agrees with this?"

"Are you kidding? Of course she's on board with this! Stephanie Stiletto will earn in one month what Michelle Dailey would earn in ten months! Can't you see yourself licking her boots?"

Browne looked at Ribaldi with a furrowed eyebrow. "No. But I'm sure someone will."

Ribaldi laughed that laugh again. "I guarantee it! I tell you, an honest-to-God jail matron turned S & M star – it'll make millions! Millions, I'm telling you! Today, the county jail! Tomorrow, Hollywood and 'Entertainment Tonight!' And then the ultimate: The Hard Rock Casino in Las Vegas! Stephanie Stiletto, winner of the AVN awards, six straight years and counting!"

Browne shook his head, and replied measuredly: "Don't do it. Don't degrade Michelle Dailey's soul to make money off of her body. What does it avail a man, or a woman, to gain a fortune and lose his or her soul?"

Ribaldi laughed louder, and clapped Browne on his shoulder. "Browne, you're a riot! The stuff you come up with! That's why I like you!"

Fortunately for Beau Browne, Ribaldi hadn't figured out how at that point to tie the performance of a Congregational pastor into his get-rich-quick scheme. And Beau had enough jailhouse moxie to get Ribaldi to pray, as part of the penitent-priest privilege, and in the midst of the prayer, the entreaty to the Almighty, to get Ribaldi to strike a deal: Beau's silence in exchange for Beau's non-participation. That may have been the only time in his life that Giovanni Ribaldi ever listened to anybody.

IX

Meanwhile, the FBI struck again, this time in Fort Worth, Texas. The media blowback from the Beau Browne case did not have any appreciable impact on the G-Men's zeal to enforce the Super Patriot Act of 2049, other than the reluctantly made agreement not to use torture "unnecessarily." Gloom, Doom and Boom didn't read the Internet newspapers, anyway. But Deacon Joe Green did. And his latest sermon featured the latest legal controversy:

"Brothers and sisters: Now, at the Calvary Jamboree we have learned to *help* our *brothers* who *need* help. But the FBI doesn't seem to have *heard* the word of the Lord. Their latest arrest for *treason*, in the so-called violation of the so-called Super Patriot Act of 2049, is Bishop Dennis Monroe of the First United Methodist Church in Fort Worth, Texas. And Bishop Monroe did the *same thing* as Pastor Browne. The *same thing!* He took in a junior high school teacher who allowed a 13-year-old boy to feel her clothed breasts on the schoolyard during recess. Yes, *clothed breasts* on the *playground*! *At recess!* For that the authorities gave her probation. But under the law of the great state of Nevada, they say she committed lewdness with a minor child, and that carries a mandatory minimum sentence of 10 years in prison to life. Now, *how* does a schoolteacher like that become an enemy of the *State*? Understand, I'm not *condoning* what she did. In fact, I think her school district should have *fired* her for doing that. But I suspect that that young boy was *not offended* in the *least* by what this teacher did. In fact, I suspect he *celebrated* with his boyhood classmates on the *playground* over his discovery of the female *breast*!

But no matter. She is an enemy of the State, even though this teacher's case didn't happen in a God-forsaken place like *Nevada*. Like Adam Kolkoski in the Brother Browne case, she *couldn't* find a job, she *couldn't* find a place to live, she attempted *suicide*, and then Brother Monroe stepped in. With his wife's blessing, Brother Monroe *took* her into his parsonage. Gave her *help* when nobody would help her. Gave her *food*. Gave her *shelter*. Found her a *job*. Gave her a *reason* to *live*! And for *this* Brother Monroe is going to prison for *life*! For life? That's right, brothers and sisters, *for life*! Our Government believes that Bishop Monroe is so unworthy for what he did that he must never enjoy the free world, *for life*!

Ah, but the FBI says this case *differs* from Brother Browne's case. They say they learned their *lesson* from Brother Browne's case and didn't water board Brother Monroe. But they also say Brother Monroe confessed anyway. Confessed? Confessed his sins? What sins? What did he confess? That he is the Good Samaritan? We, the people, claim to be Christians, but we've made it a crime to be a *Good Samaritan*? And as long as we don't water board the Good Samaritan, we can proudly call ourselves *Christians*??

I ask you, brothers and sisters, what's next? Will the FBI be looking for *sinners* at the *Calvary Jamboree*? Will they use our Fountains of *Faith* as the new Terrorist Baptismal Tank? Will my sermons soon be a thing of the *past*? Will I be *locked up* like Brother Browne and Brother Monroe? And what about *you*? Are *you* next, for following our Lord's *greatest commandment*?

If I were to tell you to send a message to Washington that you don't support the Super Patriot Act of 2049, and not to pay the 15% of your taxes that go to the Corrections Corporation of America, would that mean that the FBI would get the IRS to audit our charitable status? I would not put it past them. Therefore, I say to you: Render unto Caesar what's due Caesar; but send the money you owe to the IRS, wrapped in wrapping paper with rotten fish and moldy bread, and tell them that this is your sequester! *Your sequester*! This is how you do a 'sequester!' With money wrapped in *dead fish and moldy bread*! If our government doesn't want to help the poor, but only wants to create the poor, then *sequester Washington*! Give our government the *food* of the *poor*!! *Taxes* paid with *tilapia*! And see how the high and mighty people in Washington *enjoy that*!!

I tell you, the FBI may not believe this, but terrorists don't crawl under every *rock*! They *don't*! America's greatness *used* to lie in its security, in its knowledge that you won't *find* a terrorist under every rock! But when America gets to the point where it believes you *can* and you *will*, and it has to *pass* and *enforce* laws like the Super Patriot Act of 2049, then *we* the people get the government we *deserve*. And when we get the government we deserve, America loses its sense of *security*. And when America loses its sense of security, America loses its sense of *greatness*. And when America loses it sense of greatness, it has *no* street credibility in the world. *No street cred whatsoever*! Our overseas neighbors just see us as a bunch of *whiny bullies*! And when good men of the cloth get arrested for doing what the Lord told us to do, I for one *have had enough*! I want America to be *great again*! I don't want to live in a nation full of a bunch of *whiny bullies*! Who's with me? I'm talking to you, *television and Internet journalists*! I'm talking to you, *Republicans*! I'm talking to you, *Democrats*! Do you want

America to be great again? Would that be *okay with you*? Are you *with me*?"

Among the many who heard that sermon and fully agreed with Deacon Joe Green, one included Professor Dockett of Cornell. The First United Methodist Church of Fort Worth had enough of a donation bankroll to afford a dream team of lawyers to defend Bishop Monroe. The church picked Dockett as one of the first choices for the Dream Team.

Thus, when Professor Carter at Columbia contacted Professor Dockett at Cornell, Dockett did not appear too sanguine about hopping aboard the "Musk Mobile" and heading west. The "Musk Mobile" consisted of a nationally interconnecting set of vacuum tubes with a train that could go about 400 miles per hour, and get from New York to San Francisco in about seven and ½ hours. Dockett really didn't care to meet up with Beau Browne, his nephew and Beau's "sister-in-law."

Shortly thereafter he received a phone call from Antonio Lopez-Browne. Dockett sat at his desk in his home office, playing a video game on the split screen of his laptop, when he started talking.

"Young man, I really don't have the time to help you. Level four – terrific! 'Rocket Dockett', Old Boy, you're rollin' today, Baby! No, the Dean isn't going to be too keen about Cornell's trial practice professor spending his days out west."

"Please, Professor Dockett. We'll pay you."

"No, no. *United States v. Browne.* I know the case. Level five! Fred, you are the master! The grand master! No, money isn't the issue. Time is the issue. I don't have it."

Antonio thought fast. Sure, Bishop Monroe needed Dockett's services. But the FBI didn't torture Monroe. They used up the torture on Uncle Beau. Uncle Beau needed Dockett more than Monroe did.

"Look. How about we have a meeting by Skype next Friday." By this time, with advances in pixel resolution and image depiction, Skype operated in "real" real time, with no time delays. As of 2051 witnesses regularly testified in courtrooms by Skype from anywhere in the world, projected on to screens, and in three sharp dimensions the holograms looked exactly like real people. A witness testifying from Abu Dhabi appeared the same as a witness testifying from Alberta, who appeared the same as a live witness testifying from Albuquerque.

"Well, Fridays are the days off for the Northern District of Texas. High school football, you know. Okay, I'll be available at 4:00 your time. Don't be late, or I'll be gone. Justin F. Kimball High has quite the quarterback this year, or so they tell me!"

Antonio did his best to hide his irritation. Who cares about some stupid video game, and who cares about some stupid hotshot 17-year-old at Justin F. Kimball High? We're talking about Uncle Beau's life here! Some kid gets a scholarship to the University of Texas, while Uncle Beau gets a "scholarship" to USP Leavenworth? But Antonio and Esperanza Lopez contacted the professor on the date and time in question by Skype.

Esperanza Lopez said, "Let's quit fooling around. It's obvious what the defense of this case is: It's a First Amendment defense. Right? Beau Browne did what he did in the name of the First Amendment's freedom of religion. He's absolutely immune from prosecution."

Dockett paused periodically while clipping his fingernails with an electronic nail clipper. "Well, I'd like to agree with you. In fact, if it makes you feel any better, I do agree with you. But your Judge Hixson won't."

"What? What do you mean by that?" Demanded Esperanza.

"I mean this. Ouch! Damn it! Prior to 2014 that defense absolutely would have worked. But if you will recall from law school days, in 2014, the SCOTUS decided this case called *Burwell v. Hobby Lobby*. In *Hobby Lobby* the SCOTUS granted corporations the First Amendment right to discriminate based on the religious beliefs of their CEO's."

"So what?" asked an irritated Esperanza. "What does that have to do with the Super Patriot Act of 2049?"

"Nothing."

"Then why are we having this conversation?" replied the impatient Esperanza.

"Because of the Fourth Circuit Court of Appeals."

"We're not in the Fourth Circuit, Professor," retorted Esperanza.

"Yeah, and the state of Maryland sometimes wishes it weren't, either. If you'd just be quiet and listen for a minute, I'll explain it to you."

Esperanza wasn't used to reprimands like this. Antonio could tell from the look on her face: Esperanza suddenly hated both Skype and electronic fingernail clippers. But she let Dockett explain:

After *Hobby Lobby*, some enterprising, goofy right-brained tax protestors hatched a new theory to get out of paying income tax. They would incorporate themselves under subchapter S and declare, as the CEO's of their newly formed corporations, that their corporate religious beliefs forbade their corporations from paying income tax. Basically, they concocted a variation on the old scheme of individuals declaring themselves as nation-states under natural law, and thinking that justified the avoiding of payment of income tax since a state doesn't pay individual income tax. But this plan seemed better than that one on its face, because it had SCOTUS precedent – i.e.,

Hobby Lobby - behind it as well as subchapter S provisions for closely held corporations.

The federal courts saw through this plan up to a point. After all, does it not say in Mark 12:17 "Render unto Caesar what's due Caesar, and render unto God what's due God?" And don't tax protestors consist of just a bunch of greedy scofflaws who want to get out of paying income tax, regardless of their religious beliefs?

But the courts didn't debunk the theory completely. The courts held that individuals could incorporate and per subchapter S, treat their corporate income as personal income and thereby end up potentially not paying any tax. And certainly, per *Hobby Lobby*, these closely held corporations could act on their CEO's religious beliefs. But for that line of tax dodging to work, they would have to have in their corporate articles the specific religious tenets that justified the corporate decision not to pay income tax. The IRS not only would have the ability to audit said corporations, but also to act as religious experts and declare ecumenical bullshit on the said ecumenical bullshit. The IRS had managed to set up a cottage industry for men and women of the cloth, testifying in Tax Court as expert witnesses as to the true religious meaning of various corporate charters. The Tax Courts at times had become theological seminaries.

"This is all very entertaining," replied the exasperated Esperanza. "But what does this have to do with the Super Patriot Act of 2049 and the Fourth Circuit Court of Appeals?"

Dockett was starting to get testy. "Ms. Lopez, my dear, if you were my student at this point, you'd be at about a "C-" level. And if you don't start listening pretty soon, I will miss the start of the Justin F. Kimball game besides."

Dockett ignored the look of supreme annoyance on Esperanza's face and continued: "So let me cut to the punch line: In the initial First Amendment challenge to the Super Patriot Act of 2049 in 2050, the Fourth Circuit Court of Appeals adopted the judicial approach to tax protestors in the wake of *Hobby Lobby*: For that defense to work under Beau Browne's circumstances, Pastor Browne not only would have to take Kolkoski in for religious reasons, he would also have to point to the specific provisions in his church's charter that allowed him to do so. General Christian principles cannot suffice as a matter of law."

Esperanza reacted with scorn. "Oh, that's ridiculous. That theory makes no sense whatsoever. And why on earth would Judge Hixson follow the Fourth Circuit if he doesn't have to?"

Dockett rolled his eyes at the construction defect litigator. "You don't get it."

Esperanza started to go from annoyance to anger. Antonio well knew: Nobody would dare tell Esperanza Lopez that she "doesn't get it." Ever.

"What?" She asked sharply.

"In the first place, you have one of the most pro-prosecution judges in the country presiding on your case. Of course he's going to follow the Fourth Circuit ruling. In the second place, you're not trying your case to a jury, though I wish you good luck with that. You're trying your case to your Circuit Court of Appeals. You have to make the best record you can for that court, because your client is going to be found guilty and is going to prison for life. Sorry to be the one to tell you that, but that's how it is. Make the best argument you can on why the Fourth Circuit is full of morons. But find a way to distinguish their decision, if you can, rather than disagree with it. You see, the Circuit where you live hates 'Circuit splits.'"

"Explain that in plain English. What's a 'Circuit split'?"

Antonio could tell from his tone of voice: Esperanza was really getting on Professor Dockett's nerves by this time, and the football game probably had lasted five minutes into the first quarter by now. That quarterback probably had thrown at least one bomb that travelled 70 yards into the air from a flat-footed stance, and "Rocket Dockett" had missed it.

"A 'Circuit split' is where two circuits disagree on a point of law. It's the easiest way for the SCOTUS to grant certiorari, so that the SCOTUS can settle what the law is for all concerned. And your Circuit knows the deal: When the SCOTUS grants certiorari and holds that your Circuit is wrong Congress goes nuts. The conservative right-wing blowhards then start yelling about the liberal left-wing nut-jobs on that bench, and that it's time to split the Circuit. Then the Circuit starts getting defensive and protests to Congress. Then Congress won't approve Presidential judicial appointments to that Circuit. So the judges there become ridiculously overworked at the least. So, your Circuit will not create a 'Circuit Split,' not if there's any way to avoid it."

Antonio understood perfectly well what Professor Dockett was talking about. He had heard all about this in his "modern problems in the law" course in his third year at Columbia. "Professor," he asked, "What should we do?"

Dockett was blunt, almost cruelly so. "My advice to you two? Go to the prosecutor, get on your knees, and snivel for the best deal you can get for your client."

That ended the Skype call. Esperanza and Antonio visibly demonstrated annoyance, albeit for different reasons. Antonio didn't like the professor's advice; Esperanza didn't care for his manners. But finally, Esperanza said, "I hate to admit the old bastard is right, but he's right. Who's the prosecutor?"

"A Department of Justice lawyer named Chet Atkinson."

"Okay. Set up a meeting with me and Chet Atkinson."

X

    Esperanza took the Musk Mobile to Washington, DC and met with Chet Atkinson. She did not expect what she discovered about her adversary:

    Chet Atkinson presented himself as a very handsome, a very friendly and a very charming man. At least on the surface. He had a full head of distinguished, graying hair and very warm, piercing blue eyes. Chet graciously welcomed Esperanza in to his office, and asked her if she wanted French roast, Nicaraguan or Tanzanian pea berry pour-over from his private coffee stash.

    Chet then offered her his recipe for the smoothest latte available and advice on the best way to make espresso. With enthusiasm he introduced Esperanza to his favorite robot, which he affectionately called "Chloe". He programmed Chloe to make a perfect blend of espresso and steamed milk. Finally, Chloe made and poured a cup of the perfect latte for Esperanza. Basically, Chet charmed Esperanza.

    When Esperanza made an off-hand comment about her art collection, that comment led Chet into a discussion about which artists most influenced the direction of art pre-Picasso. When Esperanza stated her case bluntly for Monet and Dali, Chet did not disagree, but put on the table why Cezanne and Miro might arguably be worthier of such accolades. When Esperanza rolled her eyes, Chet deftly replied, "Maybe you're right. But if I were an art investor, that's what I'd invest in. But what government worker has the money or the know-how to invest in fine art, anyway?" And he tilted his head and smiled warmly at her, chuckling an eye-crinkling chuckle.

A man did not easily charm Esperanza Lopez, but she could sense his charisma. *A prosecutor with charisma. Any jury would really like this guy. This is going to be even tougher than I thought.*

Chet then pressed a few buttons, and the panels surrounding his DOJ cubicle turned into a vast moving 3-D video of the Caribbean in April. While this sight might have calmed and relaxed most visitors, Esperanza had seen too much of the Caribbean in April to be gushingly impressed. Instead, Esperanza cut through the niceties. "I've come to talk about how to settle this case."

"That's nice," said Atkinson without any trace of sarcasm and in hypnotic rhythm to the sound of the lapping sea waves. "And it's nice that you haven't been trying the case to the media. I appreciate that. We may get somewhere if you continue to soft-pedal the media."

"I know. Well, I have Deacon Joe Green to do the dirty work for me."

"Yes," said Atkinson, with a lightly hissing "s" that suggested "yes" could mean many different things. "Well, what do you have in mind?"

Esperanza proceeded to ignore the sights and sounds of the Caribbean and to state her case: "Have you seen and heard what Deacon Joe Green has said? Have you read the editorials about the case in *The New York Times*?"

Atkinson smiled. "*The New York Times*. What a shame that dusty old rag is going under. Have you heard the rumors about Fox buying them out?"

"Yes, and I don't believe them."

"I do. But what's your point?"

Esperanza was thrown off a bit. But she carried on: "*The New York Times. The Los Angeles Times. The New Republic. The Nation.* Even *The Economist* and *The Weekly Standard*, and *The National Review.* They all talk about the Super Patriot Act of 2049, about what a horrible piece of legislation it is, and about how it should be repealed."

"Yes, and personally, I agree with them, too."

Esperanza could hardly believe what her adversary had just said. "You what?"

"I said, I agree with them!"

"Great! We agree on something! So, you'll dismiss the charges, right?"

"Oh, no. I can't do that!"

Now Esperanza was really perplexed. "Oh, no? What do you mean, 'Oh, no'? You're on the wrong side of history, you're on the wrong side of public opinion, and you know it. You all but just said so right now!"

"I did, indeed. And you know what? I personally don't care!"

Esperanza practically sputtered out the words: "You don't care? You personally agree with me, yet you personally don't care??"

"No, I personally don't care. You see," replied Chet, talking theatrically with his hands, "when American history of this era is finally written definitively, the Super Patriot Act of 2049 will be but a footnote. You and I, we will be but footnotes within the footnote. Wrong side of public opinion? I think you're right. Hell, I hope some day history proves you right. But it doesn't matter."

"Huh?" Sputtered Esperanza. This conversation had become even more difficult to comprehend to Esperanza. But Atkinson explained:

"It doesn't matter. You see, I can't guarantee much about this life we live, but I can guarantee you this: First, at the end of the day, you will pay your taxes, or the IRS will make your life miserable if you don't. Second, the FBI will make sure you don't associate with bad people, or they will make your life miserable if you do. Third, the United States military will control what people overseas do, or stomp on them like the old bubble wrap from our childhoods if they don't behave. And fourth, some day your job will be taken over by a drone manufactured in India. Whether you like it or not, Ms. Lopez, someday what you and I do for a living will be obsolete. We, or our successors, will have to move to Kolkata in order to have a job. It's inevitable. Hope you can handle the humidity by the Ganges River, Ms. Lopez. And at the end of the day, one thing is for sure: Nobody will care about some guy named Pastor Beau Browne who went to prison for life for violating the Super Patriot Act of 2049."

Esperanza was stunned. She had never tried to negotiate a settlement in this way. She operated in a world of scaring the bejeebers out of the developer, concerning the certain liquidation bankruptcy he would face, not to mention the ridiculous amount of attorney's fees he would soon pay to try to avoid the inevitable, if he didn't quit avoiding reality, quit trying to misdirect the issue, listen to her and cave in now. The way Chet Atkinson had carried on, he simply did not know the meaning of deterrence in his position. He answered to nobody, and his employer and client, the United States Government, likewise answered to nobody. Certainly his employer and client would not answer to Judge Hixson, and good luck making Chet's employer and client answer to the Circuit Court of Appeals. Nobody and nothing could force Chet Atkinson to cave in. No specter of years of bloody litigation. No "parade of horribles" concerning blood-sucking lawyers who would bleed his client dry while he tried to stall the inevitable. Nothing. Esperanza Lopez would fare better bargaining with St. Peter at the Pearly Gates.

"Are you really telling me that there is no option but for the Government to seek to put Beau Browne in prison for the rest of his life?"

Some negotiators might have seen that comment as an admission of weakness. But Esperanza could readily see that Chet did not mediate. He was holding all of the cards in this hypothetical poker game, and he obviously knew it. There were no hole cards. He held a royal flush, he had all the chips, and he owned the bank. And everyone at the table knew it -- but Chet had spelled out the rules of this poker game to all concerned: "No folding." The issue concerned how benevolent he would want to be to the other side before crushing it.

"Tell you what," said Chet. "You have done a fine job in representing Pastor Browne so far, and I'm sure you'll do a fine job at trial; and there always is the possibility, however small, that the jury will like your client and will have a bunch of Deacon Joe Greens on it who will say "God curse the law!" In consideration of that, I will offer to your client that he may plead to attempted sedition. Under the U.S. Sentencing Guidelines he'll get about 262 months in prison, but I might be able to get authority from the Department of Justice to negotiate around the Guidelines and shave the sentence down to about 235 months. Your client will spend about 17 calendar years in prison on that deal; but that's better than the life sentence he'll get under the charge of treason if he goes to trial and loses. Follow this deal, and he might get out some day and be able to spend a little bit of time with his grandchildren before he goes on to the Great Hereafter."

Atkinson said those words without a single hint of malice or irony. His matter-of-factness was downright scary throughout his whole speech, right down to the prospect of having to put up with the humidity on the banks of the Ganges in order to follow one's dream job. He wasn't bluffing. He didn't have to bluff.

"How about 200 months?"

With no bluster whatsoever, Atkinson replied: "The Department of Justice will never let me go below 235 months. They've already told me so. No matter what I tell them, they'll never change their minds. They don't care about public opinion. They don't care about Deacon Joe Green. They just don't care. The case against your client is dead-bang solid. But even if it weren't, they just wouldn't care. When the Department of Justice prosecutes people for treason, it's either 235 months or it's life. That's it. It doesn't matter what the facts are. There's nothing to negotiate. It's not a matter of me saying to you 'I will crush you like a bug.' It's a matter of me saying to you, 'It's treason.' It's not a defective roof on a co-op high-rise complex in midtown Manhattan. It's treason."

Esperanza Lopez left Washington, DC in a huff. She wasn't used to a negotiating system like this, where the other side bid against itself almost arbitrarily and whimsically, and in reality there was nothing to negotiate. And while part of her wanted to go to court and kick Atkinson's ass, she thought about it and realized a major truth on the ride home on the Musk mobile: Chet Atkinson wasn't the problem. The Super Patriot Act of 2049 was the problem. She could fight the law all she wanted to; but not only would the law win, it would crush her like a fermented grape. Her job was to convey this thought to her brother-in-law, and get him to agree to a deal that would carry 235 months in prison.

She visited Beau in the county jail. She conveyed the whole conversation with Atkinson to her brother-in-law, right down to "Chloe" and the pour-over lattes. She then explained exactly why Beau had to take the 235 months, unless he really wanted to be a martyr and never see his grandchildren again.

As Esperanza went on with all of the analysis, Beau sat there silently, not uttering a sound. Finally, Esperanza looked up with some exasperation. "Well?"

"No."

"What do you mean, 'No'!" shrieked Esperanza. "Haven't you heard a word I've said?"

"Yes."

"Don't you ever want to see your grandchildren again?"

"Yes."

"So, why aren't you agreeing to the deal?"

"Because."

"Would you stop playing games with me? Stop being so coy. Why won't you take the deal?"

"I did nothing wrong."

"What?! You violated the Super Patriot Act of 2049! You harbored an enemy of the State! What do you mean 'I did nothing wrong'?"

"I did nothing wrong."

Esperanza was starting to get to the "beyond annoyed" stage.

"The law says you did! The government says you did! Judge Hixson will say you did! You are going to go to prison for the rest of your life! You will die in prison! You'll never see your grandchildren again! Do you really want to be a martyr? Is it worth flushing your life down the toilet like this?"

Pastor Browne lowered his head, looked and pointed at his sister-in-law with all of the intensity he could muster, and simply said, "I...did...nothing...wrong!"

"So, you're not going to accept my advice and plead guilty. Is that what you're saying?"

"Yes."

Esperanza was practically coming out of her shoes. In her universe, people who needed to listen to her (i.e., everybody) did so. This was a first. Well, actually, a second; Atkinson did come first. But he and Chloe didn't count right now. Her client and brother-in-law did.

"Fine. Be a martyr. See if I care. You'll have your fair trial, and when it's done, you'll go to prison for life. Just don't say I never told you so. Some day you'll say, 'Gee, I should have listened to Esperanza.' Do you get that?"

"Yes."

Esperanza grew more and more upset by her brother-in-law's cryptic nature. "So, you understand what I'm saying, you know I'm right, and yet you won't plead guilty. Is that the bottom line?"

"Yes."

Esperanza sputtered, "Is there anything else you want to tell me?"

Beau simply said, "Do your best."

Esperanza left the jail, astounded and angry. It never occurred to her that there might have been a reason her brother-in-law was not being his usual talkative self.

A few days later, Esperanza and Antonio contacted Professor Dockett by Skype:

"Well, I did what you said to do. I sniveled for a deal. And I must tell you both, Chet Atkinson is a very charming man."

"I know," replied the Professor. "That's why the DOJ chose him to prosecute this case. He's the most charming, the most personable guy they have. He is the perfect choice to prosecute a likeable defendant breaking an unlikeable law. The DOJ is banking on the proposition that the jury will like Atkinson so much that they will overlook the cause you are fighting, follow the law, and convict your client."

"I explained all of that to Beau Browne," replied Esperanza. "But he wants to go to trial. I got him a deal for 235 months, and he just won't take it. He wants to be a martyr. He's being stupid."

"Well, glory be and the saints be praised," quipped Dockett. "Here in 2051 we still live in a country where Congress and the courts haven't taken away our constitutional right to be stupid!"

Esperanza laughed. Antonio did not. Instead, he spoke up. "Professor, I thought of another angle of defense that maybe we could play."

Both Esperanza and Antonio could see Dockett's arched eyebrow on Skype, though by that time the pixel resolution of Skype allowed them to see the small scar under his chin upon looking carefully enough at him. "Go ahead," said Fred.

"Well, I know the SCOTUS held a few years ago that the FBI could use torture when they are investigating an act of terror. But isn't the law still that an involuntary confession can't be used in a court of law?"

Dockett immediately said, "Wow! Of course! The SCOTUS has never overruled *Mincey v Arizona*, even though that case was handed down in 1982!"

Esperanza interrupted: "What are you talking about? What is *Mincey v. Arizona*?

Professor Dockett arched that eyebrow. "Don't they teach you people anything in law school any more?"

Esperanza shot back, "It's been 20 years since I've been to law school, Professor! They didn't have speaking robots that hypnotized you and droned legal lectures into your brain at night in those days!"

"Oh," quipped Dockett. "Well then, don't they teach you people anything in the Bar Review cram course any more?" Dockett chuckled at his own inside-joke, and continued.

"Well, anyway, *Mincey v. Arizona* holds that when the police extract a confession out of a suspect involuntarily, the prosecution can't use the confession for any reason, not even to impeach the testimony of the defendant at trial."

"Right!" said Antonio. "So, couldn't we bring on a motion to suppress Uncle Beau's statement on the grounds that it was involuntarily coerced? Because if we win that motion, they have no other evidence from what I've seen that Kolkoski ever lived at the parsonage!"

"That's brilliant, young man!"

"No," said Esperanza sharply, "That's stupid. In the first place, they have Kolkoski's registration with the local cops. In the second place, Beau admitted that Kolkoski lived there before Gloom and Doom started torturing him. In the third place, you can bet that the government will subpoena Kolkoski to testify against Beau. In the fourth place, because the law allows torture, Hixson is going to go with that over some ancient case called *Mincey v. Arizona*. I've told you two, the First Amendment defense is the only defense available!"

Antonio felt crushed, and even over Skype Professor Dockett could sense that. So, he spoke up:

"I half agree with both of you," replied the Professor. "I agree that Hixson won't suppress the statement – and frankly, I'm not sure you want the statement suppressed completely, anyway. I mean, why suppress 'The Sermon on the Mount' and the storm troopers' responses to it? But, I think because *Mincey* and *Jackson v. Denno* from 1964 are still good law, he'll have to give a jury instruction, advising the jury that they may disregard Browne's statement if they find it was involuntarily given as the product of torture. If you give the jury an out in this case, they just might take it."

"Wait a minute," retorted an annoyed Esperanza. "Speak English. What is *Jackson v. Denno*?"

"Well," responded the sartorial professor, "Ms. Lopez, evidently both you and I are bilingual. You speak English and Spanish. I speak English and 'legalese.' So, let me educate you. *Jackson v. Denno*, decided back in the days when we had a real SCOTUS with the Warren Court, holds that even if an involuntary confession is let into evidence by the judge, the jury can ultimately decide that the confession is involuntary; and if they so decide, they are instructed to ignore it. So, what your learned son is telling you, this issue ultimately rests with the jury, which is your only hope really at trial. Is that correct, Antonio?"

"You got it, Professor!" responded a pleased Antonio.

"It won't work! I don't like it," responded Esperanza. "And I don't like you!"

Fred arched that eyebrow again. "Well, Ms. Lopez, if it makes you feel any better, you're not very high on my 'like list,' either."

"I'm lead counsel, here. I'm the general. You're the private. We do what I say."

"Well, General Westmoreland, in that case I'm headed to Vancouver."

Esperanza retorted, "I thought you were in Dallas."

"Yes, and Dallas is lovely this time of year. And you obviously haven't studied your American history, Mrs. Lopez. Antonio, I wish you all the good luck. Try to knock some sense into your father's head, if you can. Adios, Señora Lopez!" And Dockett deactivated the Skype call, before Esperanza could get in the final word.

XI

Esperanza went home, furious. For one thing, anyone who ever called Esperanza "Mrs. Lopez" or "Senora Lopez" was in for a tongue-lashing. For another, anyone who assumed she spoke Spanish like some illegal immigrant who didn't see the need or was too ignorant to learn English was in for a bigger tongue-lashing. And anyone who called her "father" or a like masculine label and denied Esperanza her femininity would never repeat that mistake again. Bonita saw the look on her wife's face, and knew this was going to be another night of the "grand tiptoe." Esperanza said a few things about that arrogant bozo professor from Cornell, mocking the name of the institution "Cornell" as she spoke. But Bonita had something else on her mind:

"Panz, how is Antonio handling all of this?"

Esperanza was stunned. She hadn't even considered the subject matter.

"I don't know. And why do I care? And why do you care? This is my case."

"I know," replied Bonita. "But Antonio is our son. I talk to Antonio all the time. This case means so much to him. It's all he talks about."

"What are you saying?"

"I'm saying, listen to him. He talked to me the other night about his Uncle Beau. He told me all of the ideas he had on how the case could be defended. And he said you just would not listen to him. He's hurt."

"Then he can just go back to the National Legal Aid Foundation and defend more people being evicted for not paying rent," said Esperanza, dismissively. "This is a huge case. I don't have time to be his mentor. If he wants a mentor, then tell him to go find someone else."

Bonita sighed. On the one hand, she so wanted Antonio to win, even more for his sake than for her brother's. But on the other, she knew what a time bomb her mate of decades was, and how she could explode at any minute. But even now, she had compassion for Esperanza and the stress level she was undergoing. Bonita had not shut down completely in spite of any and all reasons to do so.

Bonita went to touch Esperanza. Esperanza shrugged her off. "Don't touch me. I'm not interested."

"I know you're not interested in foreplay. I wasn't coming on to you. I just want you to relax, honey. Can I make you a deal? If we could just go away to the spa this weekend and have a good mud bath, would you talk to Antonio on Monday and see what he has in mind?"

Esperanza calmed down a bit. A spa mud bath didn't sound like a half-bad idea.

They went. After dipping into the mud bath, in the natural spring covered with an opened sunroof, Esperanza administered a few handfuls of mud to Bonita. At one point, Bonita giggled uncharacteristically and smeared some mud on Esperanza's upper chest. She then quickly stopped, expecting that Esperanza's breasts had some figurative barbed wire surrounding them. But Esperanza's body language did not display the usual resistance. In fact, Esperanza almost seemed to break character when she splashed some mud toward Bonita's face and likewise giggled as Bonita splashed back.

Suddenly Esperanza and Bonita had a glimpse of a reminder of when they were twenty-eight and twenty-two years old and hungered for each other's bodies. The heat from the mud bath seemed even warmer, even more inviting. The sun seemed to shine through the sunroof even more brightly. But only for that moment. Bonita did not press her luck any further, and the mud splashing stopped. Nevertheless, Esperanza came home that Sunday, almost relaxed.

     Esperanza met with Antonio the following Monday. "So, I understand you've got some ideas about your Uncle Beau's case?"

     "Yes, here's my thought: Now, we assume that Judge Hixson is going to disallow the First Amendment defense, right?"

     "He shouldn't; but I get your point. Okay."

     "Okay. But Professor Dockett told us: We're trying this case to the Circuit Court of Appeals, and we should try to distinguish the Fourth Circuit case any way we can."

     Finally, Esperanza showed some interest. Her son had addressed the subject of her defense.

     "Okay, so how do you think we can do that?"

     "Here's how. If the church's charter controls, then we call the Elders of the Congregational Church where Uncle Beau was the pastor as witnesses, and we get them to say that following the Greatest Commandment and Jesus Christ's teachings concerning the Good Samaritan is what the church's charter has always meant; and therefore, it would have been consistent with the Congregational Church, even before the Super Patriot Act of 2049, for Pastor Browne to take someone like Adam Kolkoski in to his parsonage and to offer him a job as the church janitor ."

     "That sounds like sophistry to me," responded Esperanza. Then she remembered what Bonita had said about

Antonio. "Sorry, I'm just giving you my honest opinion. You're trying to get the church to make something up after the fact in order to absolve their pastor. I doubt Hixson will go for it."

Antonio had thought it through, especially after the last Skype call with Professor Dockett. With amazing calm for such a young man dealing with his mother, much less a "Type A personality" like Esperanza Lopez, Antonio replied,

"I doubt he will, too. But here's how we get around that. We ask him for a jury instruction, that tells the jury that if they find that the Congregational Charter has always allowed Pastors like Uncle Beau to take in people like Kolkoski, then they are authorized to find him not guilty by reason of the First Amendment. That distinguishes our case from the Fourth Circuit case! And, it also gives Hixson a way to get off the hook, and let the jury throw out a case that he won't!"

Esperanza looked at her son. She could see that not only was Antonio trying to help, but also he really needed to look competent in the eyes of his mother, for the sake of his own ego. And his suggestions concerned the only defense that Esperanza had said, many times, might possibly work. And, as a matter of fact, Antonio's idea didn't sound half bad.

"Okay. Hixson may well not go for it, but we'll give it a try."

That night Esperanza came home. Bonita met her, wearing her sheer satin negligee. Bonita seemed nervous. Esperanza sensed her mate's nervousness, touched her, and said, "Let me go put on mine."

Esperanza came back, wearing her satin robe with nothing underneath. Yet, as Esperanza caressed her wife again, she could feel Bonita's tension. "What are you so afraid of? Just lie there. I'll take care of you. I always have. You know that."

As Bonita relaxed, for the first time in years the married couple made love.

As they lay there in the afterglow, Bonita started to cry.

"What's the matter?" asked Esperanza.

"Panz, this is the closest I've been to you in years. This is the happiest I've felt in years."

Esperanza paused, then said, "I know. We need to do this more often."

Bonita responded, "I agree. I have an idea. What do you think about this? Can we do this every Sunday night?"

Esperanza snapped. "Why must you be so routinized? Does that mean you have something better to do on Fridays? And if so, what is it?"

Bonita continued to cry softly. Things were never going to change after all. They never had. She knew that.

They turned their heads away from each other on their respective pillows and went to sleep.

XII

About two weeks before Beau's trial was to begin, the people of the United States of America witnessed the flying circus known as *The United States of America v. Simon Goldblatt, also known as Giovanni Ribaldi*, with the Honorable Edwin Norcross, presiding. People talked about this trial for years, much like they talked about the trials of the Chicago 7 and of the Manson family in the 1960s for years.

The performance art started during the prosecutor's opening statement. "Ladies and gentlemen, the Government is going to show you that this man (pointing at Ribaldi) engaged young girls in the production of pornography."

Immediately Ribaldi rose and interrupted. "Pornography? Pornography is about fucking! My films are not about fucking! My films are about art!"

Judge Norcross immediately warned Ribaldi: No more outbursts like that, or else he would be held in contempt of court.

Ribaldi responded: "Your Honor, is the problem here with my use of the term 'fucking'? If I say 'fornicating under the crown of the king,' am I free to express myself?"

The Judge sharply commented, "No, you're not free to express yourself!"

Ribaldi rejoined, "And I'll bet you're not, either. I mean, at your house do you ever go to your wife and say, 'Hey, Baby, let's fornicate under the crown of the king?' I didn't think so, either!"

"You're perilously close to being held in contempt, Mr. Goldblatt!"

"Fine, I'll solve both of our problems! I'll go ask her for you!"

Immediately, Judge Norcross issued Ribaldi his first citation for contempt, and a fine of $1000.

Then, the Government called the person from North Carolina who filed the complaint with the FCC. During examination, the transcript read like this:

Q: Now, Mr. Jones, did you consider "Debbie and Daria Do Detroit" to be pornography?

A: Yes.

Q: Why?

A: Well, my teenaged boy who saw it said he got an erection watching it.

Ribaldi: Erection? You say your son voted for someone in China while watching my movie??

Prosecutor: Move to strike, your Honor.

Ribaldi: How do you strike an erection?

And as Ribaldi simulated masturbation, Judge Norcross held Ribaldi in contempt. He fined Ribaldi $1000 on the spot. Immediately a buxom young woman seated in the front row of the public portion of the courtroom approached the clerk with two checks for $1000 apiece.

Next, the prosecutor had a witness describe a movie Ribaldi had made, with a teenaged male actor portraying Tarzan with a tiny, revealing loincloth. He asked the witness if he considered it pornography. The witness responded affirmatively.

Ribaldi interrupted: "That is incorrect! It's pornography only if Jane comes in on a vine from a swinging party! I'm sorry, but you lose Final Jeopardy! How much did you wager? $100,000? Oh, I'm so sorry!" And Ribaldi made that whistling sound of "Jeopardy" as the contestant's fortune turns to dust.

Again, Judge Norcross held Ribaldi in contempt. Again he fined Ribaldi $1000. Again the buxom woman seated in the front row came out with her checkbook and paid the fine.

Judge Norcross asked, "Who are you?"

The woman sweetly replied, "I'm the fine lady!"

And without missing a beat, Ribaldi said, "And she is one fine lady, lemme tellya!"

The trial went on like that. Judge Norcross held Ribaldi in contempt nine times. Each time the fine lady paid the ten bills. The US Courts made $9000 off of Giovanni Ribaldi, and he enjoyed spending every penny of it. The jury did its best to suppress laughing out loud throughout the trial. The trial became the topic of every stand-up comic, late-night television talk show host, and political blogger in the country. Some joked that former Presidential candidate Ribaldi should be made the new host of "Jeopardy," replacing the iconic but aging Ryan Seachrest.

Finally, Judge Norcross reached the limit of his patience. During closing argument the prosecutor argued about how the "Artsy-Fartsy Show" was pornography. Ribaldi blurted out: "Pornography? I make art! You make pornography! I glorify the female form! You government hacks treat women like shit! You have for decades!"

Judge Norcross had finally had it, and ordered the Marshal to tape Ribaldi's mouth shut. Ribaldi ducked the first move, and as he ran around the courtroom and leaped on to the defense table, he cried out, "Censorship! Even Hitler listened to Wagner and admired Leni Riefenstahl! Censorship! This country hates art! We're worse than Hitler!" Finally, the

Marshals pulled him off of the table, tackled him, put him on the ground and taped his mouth shut with masking tape.

And yet, through all of this, the jury found Giovanni Ribaldi not guilty. Ribaldi triumphantly left the courthouse with "the fine lady" on one arm and another lady on the other. He introduced the exotic lass to the media as Stephanie Stiletto. But it wasn't Michelle Dailey on his arm. It was some young BDSM queen with the stage name of Mistress Payne. Pornography hadn't reached the point in the mid-21st century where BDSM queens could use their real names. Meanwhile, the media crowded in and confronted the jury. Why and how did they reach their verdict?

"Because, in the end, we could not agree beyond a reasonable doubt that what Ribaldi was doing constituted pornography, as opposed to an artistic statement about the absurdity of sexual relationships in America today."

Of course, that statement became a hotbed of controversy among newspaper op-ed writers, Facebook memes, and television news and Internet commentators. Was this jury exceptionally smart or was it exceptionally naïve? Had it fallen prey to the huckster known as Giovanni Ribaldi? Had he seduced them with his charm like he seduced that 17-year-old girl?

But while the nation became involved in that debate, Antonio Lopez-Browne pondered the case, then suddenly realized that the debate spawned an entirely different issue, namely, this:

If Ribaldi's jury could decide whether his film constituted pornography or not, why couldn't Uncle Beau's jury decide whether Kolkoski was "an enemy of the State" or not?

Antonio ran the thought by Esperanza. Unsurprisingly, she snapped. "How many times do I have to explain this to you, Son? We're going with the First Amendment defense! Look, it's very simple: The statute authorizes the Department of Justice to decide who an 'enemy of the State' is. The DOJ did so. That's all we need to focus upon. Don't confuse the issue."

But Antonio thought the issue deserved more careful consideration than that. He wasn't willing to give up on the idea so easily. He spent hours in the law library, researching the law like he was on a treasure hunt, before he found his "buried treasure": A number of old 20th Century SCOTUS cases: *Sandstrom v. Montana, Sullivan v. Louisiana, and Gaudin v. United States*, all holding that only a jury could decide each and every element of the charged crime beyond a reasonable doubt, and a judge constitutionally could not tell them that they must presume an element of the charged offense has been proven without evidence or stipulation.

Antonio became excited, as only a legal nerd can. *Yes, Uncle Beau has a "First Amendment" defense; but he also has an "enemy of the State" defense! The DOJ be hanged; a jury, twelve honest and reasonable citizens of the United States, should be allowed to decide who an "enemy of the State" really is! Yes, they could hear the DOJ's opinion, courtesy of the Code of Federal Regulations, concerning the identity of an "enemy of the State"; but the jury should have the final say on the subject matter! Isn't this why we have juries? Wasn't this what the framers of the Magna Carta, much less the Constitution, had in mind? Surely at least one person on the jury with a lick of common sense will conclude that a pastor giving aid to the downtrodden cannot be "an enemy of the State," no matter what the past history of the downtrodden happened to be! Just because the wonks in the Department of Justice have a lack of common sense doesn't mean a jury of Uncle Beau's peers will likewise be just as clueless! Surely, people in the community must have heard about and/or seen the many sermons Deacon Joe Green has given on the topic,* and/or read or watched the many editorials the news media has run on the Super Patriot Act of 2049!

Antonio found himself excited, but also fearful of questioning his mother's authority. After thinking about what to do, he decided: Talk to his client. See what Uncle Beau thinks. If Uncle Beau tells them to go with an enemy of the State defense, then they have to follow his direction – whether Esperanza Lopez likes it or not.

So, Antonio went to visit his client, Uncle Beau. He described the situation to Uncle Beau in detail. When he was done, Antonio asked Uncle Beau what he wanted to do. Browne's response caught Antonio by surprise:

"Ask Professor Dockett."

"But Uncle Beau: Professor Dockett quit the defense team."

Beau responded, nodding his head and gesturing: "You, ask Professor Dockett."

Antonio left the jail, oblivious to the fact that those seven words were the only words that Beau Browne had spoken during the entire visit.

At that point, the media broke the news. In Dallas, the jury had found Bishop Monroe guilty of violating the Super Patriot Act of 2049. He now faced life imprisonment. Antonio called Professor Dockett anyway, hoping for anything that might help his client.

Dockett responded. "Well, young man, you are a thinker, I must say. Level six! *'Señor* Rocket Dockett, you are *bueno!*' No, I thought of an 'enemy of the State' defense, too, and tried it for Bishop Monroe, but the trial judge shut us down and wouldn't let us use it. I'm sure your Judge Hixson will do the same thing. But like I told you before, you're trying your case to the Circuit Court of Appeals. Damn it! Back to Level One! Fred, you've got to learn how to multi-task! No, throw that defense in there. Throw everything you can against the wall. Something might stick, who knows. Ah, Fred! You stink! Nice talking to you, Antonio. Call me any time!"

Antonio hung up with excitement, but also with fear about approaching his mother. He knew what she would say. And he knew that she would not be happy, that he went behind her back in talking with Uncle Beau and with Dockett.

Predictably, Esperanza was furious with her son. But Antonio kept his composure and said, "Mother, listen to me. There is nothing inconsistent about a "First Amendment defense" and an "enemy of the State" defense. In fact, if you think about it, they resemble each other. There is no reason we cannot present both."

Esperanza retorted, "The more defenses you put up there, the more desperate you look. Juries sense that, and the other side points it out in closing argument. We're better off with one defense. For once, trust me on this one, Son."

Antonio stood his ground. "Consider this. If we have more than two defenses, then it does look desperate. But if we have just two, and if they are pretty similar, then we try to empower the jury and say to them, 'Look! You get to decide which defense you like! It won't hurt our feelings a bit if you disagree with us on one, as long as you agree with us on the other!'"

Esperanza stopped, thought for a few seconds, and looked at her son. She knew: They both weren't wrong. And she had never tried a case like this in her career. Her son's position just might work.

"All right, Son. We'll give it a try."

Normally co-counsels don't hug each other while strategizing a case. But in this case, Antonio and Esperanza did so.

"However," said Esperanza, "You are going to have to file the motion to Judge Hixson, and you are going to have to convince him to give the jury instruction setting forth the defense."

Antonio did so, and Judge Hixson treated him to a sample of the judicial whackings to come in the upcoming trial. After Antonio argued the law and argued *Sandstrom, Sullivan* and *Gaudin* to him, Hixson pointed to Chet Atkinson and said, "Government's position?"

Atkinson suavely responded. "The Government strongly opposes the defense motion, for the reasons that the Government successfully opposed an identical motion in the *United States v. Monroe* case recently tried to a guilty verdict in the Northern District of Texas. Simply put, that defense is an invitation to jury nullification. That defense allows the jurors to ignore the law and decide for themselves what the law is, when we already know what the law is. The law is that Congress has left it up to the Department of Justice to decide who 'an enemy of the State' is. It is simply outrageous to think that twelve common people could have a better handle on who this country's enemies are than the Department of Justice!"

Hixson looked at Antonio, snarled, and said, "I agree with Mr. Atkinson. And young man, if you so much as hint in this trial that the jury can decide who 'an enemy of the State' is, I will hold you in contempt of court. And be advised right now: unlike Judge Norcross, I don't fine people whom I hold in contempt; I make them go to jail. Don't bring 'a fine lady' into my courtroom! Mention that one time in this trial, and you will be your client's cellmate! Is that clear?"

With surprising aplomb, Antonio responded, "I understand your ruling completely. All I ask is that I be able to offer proof outside the presence of the jury that my client wasn't intending any harm to the U.S. Government, and tender a jury instruction on the defense, so that I have a record for the Circuit Court of Appeals."

"Granted," snarled Hixson.

Things were looking really bleak, not only for Beau Browne, but also for Esperanza Lopez and Antonio Lopez-Browne.

November 22, 2051. The holiday season had been in full force since August. But in the homeless shelter on College Avenue – which evolved in its nickname from "The College of Hard Knocks" simply to "Hard Knoxville" – it was just another day. Another day where well-meaning people would drop off a holiday turkey, then run like hell to get out of there and avoid the lingering effects of the shelter's smell.

Into Hard Knoxville walked a uniformed US Marshal. After asking a few questions, he walked up to a gaunt man who looked to be about 85-years-old. "You Kolkoski?"

"Who wants to know?" Adam had learned over the years never to answer that question from a uniformed stranger with "Yes."

"Here. This is for you."

"What the hell is this? Am I being evicted from Fort Knoxville, too? What perverted thing did I do this time?"

"Shut up and read the piece of paper, Wise guy. It's a subpoena."

"Subpoena for what?"

"For the trial of *United States of America v. Beau Ezekiel Browne.* The Government is subpoenaing you to testify on its behalf."

Adam slowly stared at the process server with as much of a killer look as the old man could muster. "Are you telling me that our Government expects me to give them information that will lock Pastor Browne up for the rest of his life?"

"That's what it looks like, Pal. You are to meet with the FBI case agent and the trial prosecutor in his office a week before trial. They will go over your testimony with you. The subpoena tells you where the meeting place is."

About a week before the trial was to begin, the news hit the media: Adam Kolkoski committed suicide. The official story went like this: After Pastor Browne's arrest, Kolkoski became homeless again. He couldn't find a job and couldn't find a place to live. At age 67, his depression became overwhelming. On the day of the scheduled interview, instead of meeting with Atkinson to give up Beau Browne, he gave up on life. He jumped off of a freeway overpass and bounced off a driverless 18-wheeler.

Antonio went to see Uncle Beau in jail, to make sure that this news wasn't upsetting to him.

But Beau Browne said, "Talk to the prosecutor. I will plead guilty."

Antonio was stunned. Whatever he might have expected, he didn't expect this. But as smart as he was, Antonio had never experienced the feelings before of dealing with the suicide of a family member, close friend or loved one. He had no idea of the intense feeling of survivor's guilt that a suicide can create.

He also did not understand what months of being locked up could do to the human psyche. He did not understand how being stuck in county jail for seeming eternity, with no end date in sight, could cause one to give up – if for no other reason than to get out of that hell and move to a different place, even if it were a different level of hell.

But even so, the situation hit him wrong. Pastor Browne's words didn't match up with his expression or his demeanor.

"Why, Uncle Beau? You have told us from the beginning that you did nothing wrong. And I believe you. I think you did nothing wrong! Why on earth would you plead guilty?"

"Adam died because of me."

Antonio responded. "No, he didn't die because of you. He died because of a society that decided that he must not ever be forgiven. He died because of a Godless society."

Browne shook his head. "Adam died because of me."

Antonio reacted with alarm. "Uncle Beau, that's crazy! That's absolutely crazy! You were the only human being to show him kindness. If you hadn't done that, he probably would have reached the end of his rope and committed suicide at least one year earlier."

Beau shook his head again. "Adam died because of me."

Antonio stopped, and thought about how he could get through to his client.

"Uncle Beau, if it were possible to resurrect Adam Kolkoski and bring him into this jail right now, what do you think Adam would say to you?"

"You bastard."

"No. No, he wouldn't, Uncle Beau. Here's what he'd say: 'Pastor Browne, you were the only human being on earth who ever tried to make a difference to me. You showed me mercy, when nobody else would. The law in this country for years has forgotten that justice must be tempered with mercy. You have to avenge my death. And the way you do that is you stand tall. You insist that justice from hereon out be tempered with mercy.'"

Beau sat there for the longest time. His face turned red, and he breathed rapidly, shallowly, and loudly. Antonio became alarmed.

"Uncle Beau, are you all right?"

"Yes."

"Are you sure?"

"Yes."

Antonio wasn't convinced. He had heard his momma tell him the stories over the years about her brother's stoicism and steely reserve, as long as she could remember. But this reserve seemed unusually steely. And then Antonio had a brainstorm.

"Uncle Beau, I have a proposition for you. Let me go to Deacon Joe Green, and explain the situation to him. If Deacon Joe Green gives a sermon this Sunday on tempering justice with mercy, and applies it to Adam Kolkoski's situation, will you agree not to plead guilty?"

Beau Browne stopped, and pondered the question for an unnaturally long time. What was he thinking? Antonio thought he knew: Pastor Browne felt the conflict in doing right by Kolkoski, but also in doing right by his nephew. And then Uncle Beau must have remembered the stories he often told to "his favorite nephew" about 36 years prior, when his idealism helped his father, Ryan, and enabled Ryan not to give up when Ryan quite possibly would have otherwise. Perhaps Uncle Beau also remembered his father's stories about how dehumanizing the county jail experience was, and how within himself Ryan Browne had to fight the greatest fight in his life, simply to stand up for himself and not to give up. And maybe Beau remembered his oft-repeated stories about how proud he was of his father because Ryan in fact did not give up.

"Okay. I'll be listening."

Antonio contacted Deacon Joe Green's handlers. And sure enough, Beau Browne and the rest of the country heard Deacon Joe Green's sermon the next Sunday:

"Brothers and Sisters, now, my *understanding* out west is that Adam Kolkoski, this *so-called* 'enemy of the State' in the Pastor Browne matter, committed suicide! That's right! The Adam Walsh Act drove him to *suicide*. *Suicide*! Now, the Supreme Court of the United States says that the Adam Walsh Act is not '*punishment*.' Which tells me that our high court believes that justice must *never* be tempered with mercy. The supreme law of this land is that justice and mercy are *incompatible*! Now, what do I have to say to that?

Here's what I say, and I've been saying it all year: *God curse America*!!

Now, listen here: Peter the Apostle wrestled with this, over 2,000 years ago. The people who crucified our Lord, they were wrong. We know they were wrong. Everyone accepts the *proposition* that they were wrong. But Peter preached to all to temper justice with *mercy*. Why? Because eternal *salvation* is more important than what we think is justice on earth. 'Blessed are the merciful, for they will be shown mercy!' *Peter said this*! 'And it shall be that every soul that does not heed the prophet shall be utterly destroyed from the people.' Read Acts 3:23! That's what he *said*! Or read Micah 6:8. "What does the Lord require of you? To act justly and to love *mercy* and to walk humbly with your *God*!"

It's what we do at the 'Calvary Jamboree' every day! We extend *mercy* to people like Adam Kolkoski, so that when they are ready to pass they *know* they are ready to meet the *Father*! And maybe, just maybe, Brother Kolkoski will know, as he reaches the Pearly Gates, that one man on earth, *one man*, Brother Beau Browne, extended mercy to him. And because of that, he could *leave* this earth – regardless of *how* he left it –

better prepared to meet the Father. *That's* why we extend mercy to those *surrounding* us.

But a justice system that does not allow us to show such *mercy*? A system of justice that rewards *vengeance* over *mercy*? A system of justice that *panders* to a bunch of narrow-minded *people* who believe our country is nothing more than a *junkyard of souls*? A system of justice that assumes that redemption isn't *possible*, that obedience to the commands of God isn't *possible*? A system of justice that holds that vengeance should crush mercy like a baby *spider*? A system of justice that assumes that Godless people know *best*? Godless, you say? *Godless, I say*! When we decide who may deserve mercy and who never can have it, then we have become Godless. We have become the opposite of the Good Samaritan! Once again, I must say, Brothers and Sisters: *God curse America!*"

Antonio visited his uncle the day before the trial was to begin.

"Well?"

Pastor Browne simply smiled at his nephew, and held his right thumb up. "Do your best."

XIV

At the beginning of jury selection, Judge Hixson directed the clerk to direct the prospective jurors to raise their collective right hands and swear that they would answer the questions posed completely, honestly and accurately. All of the venire except one raised his or her right hand before saying, "I do." The Clerk noticed the omission, and immediately advised Judge Hixson, "Your Honor, Potential Juror number 25 has not raised her right hand."

Potential juror number 25 was a native Serbian, emigrated to and naturalized in America, with the Anglicized name of Ana Katich. Antonio, Chet Atkinson, Esperanza Lopez and Judge Hixson took one look at her, and each became instantly captivated.

She had that effect upon a lot of men and gay women. Ana Katich was about 30-years-old, 5'7" tall, about 120 pounds, with long black hair, full lips, large breasts, an hourglass figure, long legs, and dark, piercing eyes.

Judge Hixson stated: "Ms. Katich, when the jury asked you to raise your right hand and take the oath, you refused. Why?"

Ana looked at the surly old man with those Eastern European eyes, and responded: "Your Honor. Your question assumes that I am a liar by nature, but if I put my hand on some book of yours, that somehow I am magically changed into one who can only tell the truth. I don't believe that. I believe in God. But I also believe that I was born and raised by my family to tell the truth always. I don't need to pretend to believe in God in order to tell the truth. If I tell you something outside of this courtroom, it's the truth. If I tell you something inside of this courtroom, it's the truth. Nothing changes. Raising my right hand doesn't change a lie into the truth. And raising my left hand doesn't change a lie into the truth, either."

Hixson said, "Counsel, approach the bench." Atkinson, Antonio and Esperanza did so. Hixson leaned over, "Not only am I not striking this juror from the panel, but if any of you challenge her, I'll hold you in contempt of court!"

That was the only time during the trial that the judge and all three lawyers laughed out loud at the same time.

But then, Judge Hixson asked if anyone was familiar with the case. Up went about 100 hands. He then asked if anyone had formed an opinion as a result of what s/he had read. Most of the 100 hands remained in the air. Then Judge Hixson said, "Do you mean to tell me that you people are so narrow-minded that you couldn't possibly set aside your opinions?" Oops. Down went half the hands. But only half. And of those whose hands remained, Judge Hixson excused them immediately for cause.

This was Antonio Lopez-Browne's first jury trial, and it was Esperanza Lopez' first criminal jury trial. Atkinson had already tried over 100 criminal jury trials for the Government, and he immediately became concerned for Beau Browne. Atkinson knew he had the law on his side, and as long as Hixson followed all of the rules of due process, Chet would get the Government's conviction and life sentence, and the Circuit Court of Appeals would uphold it. And he also knew that Hixson would agree with him, whenever a serious controversy presented itself. But he also knew that the combination of

Hixson, Antonio and Esperanza could screw this trial up so badly that the Circuit Court of Appeals could end up reversing the conviction. Atkinson had to make sure that Browne received his fair trial, and competent assistance of counsel was part of the fair trial the Constitution entitled him to receive.

"Your Honor," said Atkinson, "I'm concerned about a jury selection process, especially in a case as heavily publicized as this one, where all you have to do is raise your hand, or not, and you automatically get out of jury duty or you don't. I think we need to bring those people back, and we need to have individual voir dire of each person on the potential jury, away from the others, so that anything one person says doesn't affect the thinking of the rest of the people listening. We need to ask more probing questions of the jury to make sure they really can or really can't set aside their opinions. We don't know how strongly those people hold those opinions or, for that matter, what those opinions are."

Hixson scowled at Atkinson. Why on earth was this prosecutor acting like a defense lawyer? But he knew Atkinson was right. So, from that point on the voir dire examination went individual by individual, away from the others.

When it came time to examine Ana Katich, the transcript of the voir dire examination went like this, with Chet Atkinson asking the questions:

Q: Ms. Katich, can you be fair to the government?

A: What do you mean by 'fair'?

Q: I mean, can you set aside your opinions and decide this case based on the evidence?

A: Why do you think I have opinions on this case?

Q: Well, that's a good question. Do you have opinions about this case?

A: Yes.

Q: What are they?

A: Why do they matter?

Q: I'm sorry, what do you mean by that?

A: I mean, I have opinions about the law. Is that what you are getting at?

Q: Well...yes, as a matter of fact.

A: My opinion is that the law is corrupt.

Q: In other words, you can't be fair.

A: No, you did not listen to me. I did not say I could not be fair. I said that my opinion is the law is corrupt.

Q: I'm sorry. I'm really not following you. How can you be fair to the Government if you think the law is corrupt?

A: Because empires fall when the law becomes corrupt. The Roman Empire fell when the law became corrupt. The British Empire fell when the law became corrupt. The United States of America has been an empire for over 100 years. But the American Empire is falling because the law has become corrupt.

Q: Well, then, does that mean you will find Beau Browne not guilty because you think the law has become corrupt?

A: No, you do not understand.

Q: Well, you're right there, Ms. Katich. What don't I understand?

A: If the American Empire is falling because the law has become corrupt, then it is preordained. It has been predetermined. I, Ana Katich from Serbia, cannot change that. You assume that I think I can. I know I cannot.

Q: Ah! So you're saying now that you can be fair!

A: No, I did not say that. I asked you: 'What do you mean by fair'?

Atkinson sighed. "I already asked you that. I sense we are talking in circles."

Ana Katich from Serbia replied: "And you are correct. I answered that question and we are talking in circles, because I gave you an answer you did not want to hear."

Judge Hixson interrupted: "Look, just answer this simple question: Can you decide this case based only on the evidence and the instructions you hear in this case?"

Ana then asked: "What do you mean by instructions?"

The judge went on: "I mean that at the end of the trial I will give you the law as you are to apply it to the facts. You are going to apply the law, and only the law I give you, in determining whether Beau Browne is guilty or not guilty, aren't you?"

The judge said this in a way to intimidate Ana. But nobody could easily intimidate a 21st century Serbian woman.

"If you give me corrupt law, I will apply it to the facts. I told you, the corruption of the law and the downfall of the American Empire are pre-determined. But if that happens, I will tell you later exactly why the law is corrupt. If you ask me to, that is. I doubt you would ask Ana Katich from Serbia for her opinion about that. But if you do, if my opinion really matters, I will tell you what it is. And you will not like my answer. But my answer won't change anything."

Antonio asked if he could ask a question. Esperanza showed a look of annoyance, as did Judge Hixson, but both said, "Go ahead."

Antonio responded: "Ms. Katich. Let's suppose that you conclude that the law is in fact corrupt. But let's also suppose that you find, within that corrupt law, a way to find Beau Browne not guilty. Would you in that instance find Mr. Browne not guilty?"

At last, to Ana, an attorney who appeared to make some sense. "Of course."

From that point on, Antonio sensed that every time the juror, Ana Katich, locked eyes with him, she could see more than just the brown color of his irises.

XV

After opening statements, Gluck took the witness stand. Atkinson called Gluck to testify to Pastor Browne's admission regarding harboring Kolkoski. Esperanza decided that Antonio could do the honors of cross-examining the G-man, since Gluck's testimony had nothing to do with the First Amendment defense. Antonio anxiously started in, having rehearsed his cross *ad nauseum*:

Q: Isn't it true, Agent Gluck, that when you first entered Pastor Browne's parsonage, you were prepared to torture him?

A: No.

Q: But you were prepared to torture him if he didn't admit he was an enemy of the State, correct?

A: Yes, the law authorizes us to do that.

Q: Yes, the law authorizes you to do that, when you haven't decided whether to prosecute a suspected enemy militarily or in civil court. Correct?

A: What are you getting at?

Q: What I'm getting at is this: When you entered Pastor Browne's parsonage, you knew that there wasn't going to be any sort of military tribunal, correct?

A: That hadn't been decided.

Q: Is that right? Are you a military police?

A: No.

Q: Did you consult with anyone from the military before deciding to interrogate Pastor Browne?

A: No.

Q: Was Pastor Browne a member of the military?

A: No.

Q: Does the US Military own the Congregational Church?

Gluck leered at young Antonio.

A: Not yet.

Judge Hixson and some of the jury laughed. Antonio did not, and forged on.

Q: So, if Pastor Browne is a civilian, and if you are not a member of the Military Police and you weren't working with the Military Police or the JAG, then this was not going to be a military case at the time you interrogated Pastor Browne. Correct?

Gluck stumbled verbally. It felt like Antonio was on to something.

A: That's correct.

Q: And yet, you thought it was perfectly permissible to use torture against this civilian?

Atkinson finally spoke up. "Your Honor, I object and I move to strike this entire line of questioning. The law is that when interrogating a suspected enemy of the State, the police – be it the FBI or be it Military Police – are permitted to use torture. This line of questioning is both irrelevant and prejudicial to the Government."

Hixson reflexively said, "Sustained."

Antonio showed remarkable poise. "Your Honor, May we be heard on this outside the presence of the jury?"

So, Hixson had the jury put on their virtual reality helmets with inner movie visions of GI's cheering from the remotest parts of the middle East while watching the Super

Bowl, and headphone-style sounds while listening to "The Anvil Chorus" from Verdi's *Il Trovatore*, and instructed the jury to keep their heads down, while the attorneys argued.

"Your Honor, the problem is this. Nothing in the Roberts Court decision regarding torture overrules either *Mincey v. Arizona* or *Jackson v. Denno*. As you know, those cases are so old that they have been built into stock jury instructions that federal courts throughout the country have given for decades. The jury can decide whether a defendant's statement is involuntary, and if they so decide, then they can ignore it."

Atkinson knew he didn't have to say much. "Your Honor, my opponent has a point. But the Roberts Court said what they said."

Antonio responded: "That they did, your Honor. But in dicta in that case, they also said that if the US Government initially decides to prosecute a suspected terrorist in civilian court rather than in a military tribunal, and ultimately does so, then civilian law binds them. That would mean that precedent such as *Jackson* v. *Denno* binds the Government in this case. The jury should be allowed in a civilian trial to ignore an involuntary confession, even if it can be admitted into evidence."

Atkinson had nothing to say in response, and neither did Hixson. They looked at each other as if to say, "Help me out, here!" But neither one could and neither one did. Antonio knew he had checkmated both of them. Hixson took a quick recess, read the Roberts Court case, came back on the bench, and changed his ruling. He overruled the objection, and allowed Antonio to carry on.

Antonio went on, and asked Gluck about the waterboarding process. Gluck described it with a reasonable degree of matter-of-fact enthusiasm. Then Antonio pulled out his copy of the Holy Bible and read "the Sermon on the Mount" directly from Matthew 5. As he read each of Jesus Christ's commands, Gluck admitted that Pastor Browne indeed said those words. When Antonio finished that part of the cross-examination, he looked at the jury, and immediately caught the eyes of Ana Katich.

Antonio could not then have understood that during this cross-examination, Ana's eyes had captured the images in her brain of her family's oft-repeated stories. As she heard what the FBI put Beau Browne through, she remembered the stories. Her great-grandfather suffered torture in the 1940s by the Ustase at Jasenovac. Her grandfather also suffered torture in the great Civil War of Yugoslavia of the 1990s (gradjanski rat) by the Croats. Her family expressed profound bitterness toward the US Government's inability to stop it. She remembered the stories of how international refugee workers took in her grandfather and removed him and his family, ultimately to the United States for safekeeping.

Antonio may not have known any of that, since both prosecution and defense somehow neglected to ask about it during voir dire. But he did feel from the look in Ana's eyes that he had at least one sympathetic juror on Uncle Beau's side.

The next witness was an FBI Special Agent who produced the sex registry record, establishing that Adam Kolkoski had listed the parsonage address as his residential address.

Esperanza took over the cross-examination, as this testimony led into the First Amendment defense:

Q: Agent, did you actually go to the parsonage?

A: No.

Q: So, you don't know for a fact that Adam Kolkoski lived there, do you?

A: Not for a fact.

Q: In fact, isn't it true that sex offenders sometimes will give false addresses to the authorities?

A: I've heard of that happening, yes.

Q: And you have no way of knowing, personally, whether Adam Kolkoski gave you a false address or not. Am I right?

A: You're right.

Good job, Counselor. Now to destroy this guy:

Q: In your investigation into this matter, did you look to find the bylaws of the Congregational Church in question?

A: No.

Q: How about the charter of that church? Did you ever attempt to obtain a copy of that?

A: No, I didn't.

Q: Do you even know what the tenets of that church are?

At this point, Chet Atkinson interrupted. "I object your Honor. This is irrelevant, and prejudicial to the Government."

"Sustained."

Esperanza Lopez couldn't believe her ears. "What?? I demand a hearing outside of the presence of the jury, right now!"

Back went the helmets with the jurors' heads down, this time with the first movement of Orff's *Carmina Burana* playing in the heads of the jurors and the 1991 Navy Seals invasion of Iraq dancing before their eyes. Esperanza continued:

"Your Honor, we're entitled to explore this area of defense."

"No you're not, counsel. The Fourth Circuit is against you, and from what I understand, Bishop Monroe didn't fare too well with this line of defense recently in the Northern District of Texas."

"Your Honor, as I read the Fourth Circuit's opinion, if the church's charter or by-laws permit the presiding minister or priest to harbor someone, then he is immune from prosecution."

With "faux patience" Hixson replied: "That's true, counselor. But that's your defense. Immunity is a defense. You have the burden of presenting evidence on that. You can't prove a double negative through a government witness!"

Esperanza was getting testier with the crusty old judge. "Your Honor, the defense never has the burden of presenting evidence on anything!"

The level of their voices caused some of the jurors to stop listening to *Carmina Burana*, take off their helmets, and hear the drama going on in the courtroom:

Hixson sneered at the clearly ignorant defense lawyer. "Really, Ms. Lopez? If you were to present an insanity defense, do you think you would have no burden whatsoever to establish that your client is insane?"

If Esperanza were well versed in this area of the law, she would have responded, "That's completely different your Honor. Let me explain why. The rules of the insanity defense have no analogy to anything else in the law." Instead, she spoke the truth: "I don't know."

Hixson sneered at her. "You don't know? You *don't know*?? Here your client is facing a life sentence, and he's represented by a lawyer *who doesn't know*??" Then Hixson bellowed at her: "You *have* to *know*!! You *can't not know*!!"

By this time all of the jurors had taken off their helmets without the court services officers' approval, and were staring at Hixson and Esperanza. But Hixson continued to rage: "I can't have incompetent lawyers taking up space in my courtroom!! You are presenting an affirmative defense, and you have to present witnesses to prove your defense! You can't prove it through this government witness! Objection sustained!"

Nobody talked back to Esperanza Lopez like that. "Your Honor, you are wrong! You are the one who doesn't know the law! I can prove my point however I care to prove my point!"

One could chalk up what Hixson did next to being a cantankerous old octogenarian. But truth be told, he had always had an abiding distaste for criminal defense lawyers, for women lawyers, for gay lawyers and for Hispanic lawyers, and Esperanza Lopez fit the bill on all four.

"I've had enough out of you and your attitude! Marshal, tape her mouth shut!"

The jury saw the scene, and quite naturally reacted with horror. Esperanza Lopez screamed blood-curdling screams while two Marshals put her on the ground and wrapped her mouth shut with masking tape.

Antonio had the presence of mind to shout out: "Objection! Objection! You just did that in front of the jury, with the jury's helmets off and with their knowledge! Objection!"

Hixson then turned to Antonio. "Overruled. Counsel, proceed with cross-examination."

Antonio looked like a dancer on stage in front of an audience, who had just been told his fly was down. He felt the familiar dream-state terror of showing up for final exams without ever having opened a book or attended a class. As he sat there paralyzed, Atkinson's horror rose. Atkinson really didn't want to try this case twice, and Hixson just managed to make that an extreme possibility if Atkinson didn't act really fast.

"Your Honor, in light of the fact that everybody saw what just happened, including and especially the jury, may I humbly request that we take our evening recess now, have the jury instructed to put the last half an hour out of its mind now, and have a hearing about this outside of the presence of the jury first thing tomorrow morning?"

If Antonio had made that request, Hixson probably would have snarled, "Denied." But on Atkinson's request, Hixson stated, "Granted."

The night loomed very dark and emotionally stormy.

XVI

That evening, the tension rose to dangerous heights in the Lopez-Browne household. Esperanza ranted and screamed like a woman stung by a nest of very angry wasps. Both Bonita and Antonio had never seen Esperanza so out of control.

Finally, at the fever pitch of her rant, Esperanza went off: "I quit! I've had it! I never should have taken this case! I'm done!!"

Antonio immediately showed a wide-eyed look of alarm. "Mother, are you telling me that I have to take over Uncle Beau's case and try it by myself?"

"That's exactly what I'm telling you! Tomorrow you can go to court, while I draft up a judicial discipline complaint against that senile old judge!"

Antonio responded frantically. "Mother, first of all, the judicial discipline commission has no jurisdiction over a federal judge. The only body that could get rid of him is Congress. Hixson is a senior judge. You say he's senile, and I think you're right."

Esperanza added: "Yes! I suspect he may be about two years away from assisted living!"

Antonio replied quickly: "But here's the thing: If that is true, I would think Congress wouldn't be the least bit interested in investigating a judge like that!"

Antonio had it right, and that only made Esperanza angrier. She responded:

"Then I will prepare a petition. I will go get a lot of attorneys in this town to sign it. And I will deliver it to Judge Hixson, demanding that he retire right now. I can't try this case and do that at the same time, and I think I will serve the cause of justice better if I work on the petition!"

In a pleading voice bordering on whining, Antonio said, "Mother, why can't you wait until after the trial before you do that?"

With each word, Esperanza's voice became shriller: "Because that man is a menace! He needs to be stopped now!! He needs to understand that he can't call me incompetent in front of a jury and he can't have my mouth taped shut, ever!!"

Antonio displayed a look of horror in his eyes. He felt the terror of being stuck, in the biggest jury trial in the country and his first jury trial in his career, trying this case by himself. Bonita heard the tone of her son's voice and saw the look in her son's eyes, and knew what he was thinking.

Then something inside of Bonita, after all of these years, came to the surface. Too late, perhaps; but finally, it got there. Bonita had never stood up for herself in front of Esperanza in all of those years of marriage. But the issue didn't concern her. The issue concerned Antonio.

"Panz," said Bo. Esperanza shot her a look of extreme anger.

"What did I tell you about using that name in front of Antonio?"

Bonita Browne, at long last, snapped. She had crested over the top. The firecracker inside of her finally, finally had detonated. Bonita took a breath, then addressed Esperanza, wagging her finger at her wife:

"I don't care what you told me about using that name! You are 'Panz' and you will listen to me! Your son needs help! If you want to be a selfish bitch to me, then be a selfish bitch to me! You've been doing it for years; why stop now? But don't you dare be a selfish bitch to Antonio. Antonio needs your help! Help your son! Quit thinking about yourself all the time, and just help your son!"

By the end of her speech Bonita was in tears, but they didn't last for very long. Esperanza came over to her, grabbed her hair, gave her two hard open-handed slaps across the face, yelled through her clenched teeth, "Shut the fuck up!!" and threw her wife to the floor.

And the firecracker inside of Antonio detonated as well. He grabbed Esperanza, threw her on the couch, and yelled, with a murderous look in his eyes: "Stay there! Just stay there!! Don't move!!!"

Antonio then grabbed Bonita's arm, marched her into the bedroom, and shouted, "Pack your bags! Right now!! Go!! This is it!! Just do it!! Pack your bags!!!"

Everyone in the Lopez-Browne household, even the family cat, froze. Neither Bonita nor Esperanza had ever seen Antonio act like this before. For that matter, Antonio had never seen himself act like this before. After the initial shock in the house wore off, Bonita and Antonio furiously packed her suitcase with all of the clean clothes she could find. Antonio grabbed his momma's arm, holding the suitcase in his other arm, and marched her out of the Lopez-Browne house into his car. From there he Googled the name and called on his cell phone, got the directions, and the car drove straight to the nearest battered women's shelter.

Antonio burst through the door, confronted the front office manager like that person was part of the Bonita-Esperanza conspiracy of silence, and shouted, "My name is

Antonio Lopez-Browne! This is my momma, Bonita Browne! This woman is a victim of domestic violence! Look at her face! Just look at it!"

Antonio grabbed his momma's cheek, so as to highlight the redness to the front-desk clerk. He continued his rant: "I just saw the abuser! The abuser is my mother! I just saw my mother hit my momma! My mother's name is Esperanza Lopez! My mother has been doing this to my momma my whole life!! I am 32-years-old! Don't you tell me a gay woman can't abuse another gay woman! I am sick of that lie!! I'm sick of you people discriminating against gays!! You will take her in, right now, or so help me, God, I will sue!! I'm in the middle of the most important trial in the United States of America right now, but this is more important!! I will stop the trial, and I will sue your ass!!"

The office manager stood there, dumbfounded. "You don't have to sue, sir. Welcome, Mrs. Browne!"

Antonio appeared before Judge Hixson at 8:00 am, about seven hours later. He hadn't slept. He didn't need sleep. The adrenaline had not slowed down even a wee bit. He told Judge Hixson what had happened that night. Hixson actually had a wee bit of sympathy. But only a wee bit. He gave Antonio a two-hour continuance to calm down, before the trial resumed.

In that two-hour time, Antonio desperately called Professor Dockett. He begged Dockett to come on board and help him.

Dockett responded: "Young man, I'm still trying to get over Bishop Monroe's guilty verdict. It's the first jury trial I've lost in twenty years. I understand you're upset, and I feel sorry for your situation. But I really don't have the appetite to drop what I'm doing now, abandon my students again and catch more hell from the dean, and come back out your way to lose my second trial in a year!"

"Please, Professor Dockett, please. I know you come from a place where advocacy and persuasion are incompatible with begging. But I'm begging you, sir. I can't try this case by myself, especially not today. If I can convince Judge Hixson to give me a one-week continuance, will you come out west and help me? Please? Please?"

Dockett paused. On the one hand, the Monroe verdict had taken the fire out of his belly like the world's biggest Tums tablet. The thought of fighting another unfair fight against an unjust law in front of a Nazi-esque judge sounded like as much fun as a trip to the dentist for a double root canal. Fred Dockett had accomplished many things in his lifetime; but "the king of masochism" somehow had never made its way on to his resume.

But on the other, whom did Fred Dockett idolize? Thurgood Marshall, for one. Thurgood Marshall, who won for Mrs. Brown with the enduring principle of "separate but equal is unconstitutional" in *Brown v. Board of Education of Topeka, Kansas.* How did he accomplish that, when 24 years earlier he couldn't get into the law school of his choice because of his race? Thurgood Marshall, who successfully sued that law school years later, even before the SCOTUS decided *Brown v. Board of Education*, for doing the same thing to a fellow Black man, Donald Murray. Thurgood Marshall, who brought voting rights to his people in 1944, when he convinced the SCOTUS to strike down the "whites only" voting law in Texas. Thurgood Marshall, who as a SCOTUS Justice years later authored the opinion that struck down the death penalty law that had been arbitrarily enforced.

If he were alive today, what would Thurgood Marshall do in this case? Dockett knew what Marshall would do: He'd put his butt on the seat of the Musk mobile and he would hustle out west to help this poor neophyte kid fight this unjust case. And he would find a way to win it, too, by God.

"All right, Antonio. Buy us a week of time, and I'm on board."

Now to sell it to Hixson.

But Hixson didn't care to buy. "Young man, we spent all this time picking this jury. And I'm not about to inconvenience them. I never have inconvenienced a jury in my career, and I'm not about to start now. This jury has waited around long enough today. You look like you could use a little sleep. I'll let you take a nap, and be ready to go at 1:30!"

Chet Atkinson immediately assessed the situation. He asked for the continuance the day before because of the shock of Hixson's behavior toward Esperanza Lopez. He thought that a bit of cooling off might allow him later to argue to the Court of Appeals, when the inevitable appeal would happen, that the sideshow didn't prejudice Beau Browne. And here was Hixson, doing his best to make the sideshow the main show.

"Your Honor," said Atkinson, "The Government's position on this issue is as follows: The Government is very concerned about the Defendant's right to a fair trial. Based upon what has gone on, the Government does not believe that someone in Beau Browne's position can effectively be represented by anyone who has never tried a jury trial before, much less a rookie who is as frazzled as Antonio Lopez-Browne appears to be right now. I fear that this case could be infected by structural error if the request for continuance is denied, and the Circuit Court of Appeals would reverse any conviction that would happen, no matter how strong the evidence is. Therefore, the Government joins in the request for continuance, and stipulates that the trial be continued for one week and that Professor Dockett be permitted to join Antonio Lopez-Browne as co-counsel of record."

Hixson looked at both lawyers with a big stink-eye. He said nothing for about ten seconds. Both Antonio and Atkinson wondered: Is Hixson here mentally?

Finally, Hixson spoke: "Continuance granted. Bring in the jury."

The Court Services Officer brought the jury in to open court. Hixson spoke:

"Ladies and gentlemen of the jury: This has been an historic occasion. Yesterday you saw the antics of one of the most incompetent lawyers this Court has ever seen in this Court's 45 years of being on the bench."

Atkinson winced. Hixson didn't seem very determined to correct his mistakes. But Hixson continued:

"The bottom line is that Ms. Lopez has done the first sensible thing she's done all trial: She has quit representing the Defendant. Now, this young man, Antonio Lopez-Browne, is doing a fine job for his client. A fine job. But it's his first jury trial. Under the circumstances, justice would be best served by having an experienced attorney come in and help Mr. Lopez-Browne. So, we will have a one-week continuance, so that the lawyer can get up to speed, and we will then resume the trial. Good luck, enjoy your week off, and do not talk to anyone about this case or pay attention to any media account of this case, either. We'll see you a week from today at 9:30 am."

Antonio Lopez-Browne and Chet Atkinson left the courthouse, relieved, albeit for very different reasons.

But as he left, Antonio caught the eye of Ana Katich. Ana smiled at Antonio. The beautiful young Serbian woman seemed to send Antonio a message: Everything would ultimately work out. It all would end up okay. Antonio smiled back. Then they both realized that they had better stop. So they simultaneously turned their heads, while thinking the same thing: *Woooo.*

XVII

The next morning Professor Dockett hopped on the Musk mobile and made it out west. After studying the daily transcripts of the first part of the trial, the two started to strategize the rest of the defense:

"Professor, I have had an idea but I was afraid to say it before because I knew how my mother would react. But she's gone, so here goes: What if I were to go to the Elders of the Congregational Church where Uncle Beau was the pastor, and get them to sign a proclamation?"

"A proclamation? What are you talking about?"

Antonio continued. "A proclamation that would say that from the day the church was first chartered, giving aid to the unfortunate who cannot find work or shelter was consistent with Matthew 22:39 and Luke 10:25-37, and guided the church's teachings, missions and goals."

Professor Dockett replied, "Well, Mr. Lopez-Browne, I see you have studied your Bible. That's good, I suppose. But why would you do that, exactly?"

Antonio replied, "Because then we could distinguish the Fourth Circuit case in that way, like you said we needed to do, and establish the First Amendment defense."

Professor Dockett shook his head. "It won't work. Hixson is not going to let the church Elders change their charter after the fact so as to clear their leader of the charge."

Antonio had thought it through, however. "I know, that's what Mother said, and she wouldn't listen to me. But here's how I think we can get around that."

"You have a way to get around that? Go ahead, I'm listening."

Antonio finally felt the courage to share his ideas. "Well, I've done some studying on this. When the courts hold what a non-procedural statute means, the holding applies retroactively to the day the statute was passed, unless the holding is so unforeseeable that it becomes a 'new rule.' It seems to me that the same principle should apply here to a church charter. After all, a church charter is like a statute, right? Both set forth the basic principles that the people abiding by them must follow, right? So, if the Elders say that the principle has been around as long as the church itself – and I have a solid gut feeling they will say that – then the principle should apply retroactively to the day the church was first chartered!"

Dockett scratched his head. "Wow, Antonio! That is brilliant! An 'A' for you! But there is one problem."

"What?"

"Atkinson will object, Hixson will sustain the objection, and down the tubes will go your theory of a First Amendment defense."

But Antonio had thought it through to the next level. "If we were asking Hixson to throw the whole case out on that basis, I think you're probably right. So, we don't do that. We use that evidence to support a jury instruction that says that if the jury finds that the Congregational charter has always meant that its pastor can give aid to any unfortunate in housing him and employing him, no matter what, then they can find him not guilty. I think he has to give that instruction! After all, the rule of law is that a defendant is entitled to any and all jury instructions that the evidence supports, no matter how weak or incredible that evidence may be!"

Professor Dockett stood up. "Brilliant! Brilliant! Brilliant! I think that will work! I like it! And that will allow Hixson to put it into the lap of the jury, and that will get him off the hook and ensure that he be named 'prosecutor of the year' for the tenth year! All right, go to your uncle and ask him the names of that church's elders, if you don't already know them, and get the proclamation. And be ready to argue the point to Hixson, just like you have to me!"

And that's what Antonio did. Browne gave him the name of the Elders. When Antonio went to visit them, he was quite shocked. They had the proclamation already in hand. In fact, they had drafted it two days after Gloom and Doom water boarded and arrested Pastor Browne. They asked Antonio what took the defense team so long to ask them for the proclamation. This was perfect! The Elders acted on their own, without any advice whatsoever from the lawyers representing Beau Browne! How could Hixson legitimately call this "sophistry"?

Antonio sheepishly grinned at them and said, "Better late than never!" There was no point in embarrassing his mother, Esperanza Lopez, to a group of holy men.

Antonio came back, excited, with proclamation in hand. Dockett profusely congratulated his young mentee. Antonio then said, "I have another brainstorm!"

"What?"

"All right. Something you didn't know is this: I already made a motion to instruct the jury on the 'enemy of the State' defense. Atkinson objected, and not only did Hixson sustain the objection, but threatened to hold me in contempt and throw me in jail if I ever raised it."

"Oh, Lord," responded Dockett. "That's so funny. That idiot judge in Dallas did the same thing to me in the Bishop Monroe case!"

Antonio asked intensely, "Did Bishop Monroe testify?"

Dockett responded, "No. What's your point?"

Again, Antonio showed that he had thought it through. "As I understand it, a defendant has the Constitutional right to testify. So, a trial judge can't stop a defendant from taking the witness stand."

"That's true, but I wouldn't…"

"Right. And we've already won the battle on the jury instructions for torture and involuntary confessions, and we've already got into evidence that Uncle Beau was saying the Sermon on the Mount to Gloom and Doom as they were waterboarding him."

"Okay, so what's the brilliant plan, again?"

"So, you take the examination of Uncle Beau, since you weren't here when Hixson threatened to hold me in contempt. Because he never told you anything like this, so you didn't know. And you ask Uncle Beau 'Why did you recite the Sermon on the Mount to the FBI Agents'? A legitimate question to ask, right? And Uncle Beau on cue will say, 'because I wanted to get across to the FBI that I am no more an 'enemy of the State' than Jesus Christ himself!"

Dockett looked at his mentee, sort of puzzled. "How does that help us?"

"It helps us in two ways. First, it gives us the evidence to support the giving of the 'enemy of the State' jury instruction that Hixson has already said he's going to reject. Second, maybe just maybe it gets the jury thinking. Maybe the jury will hear that and realize they don't have to go along with how the DOJ defines what "an enemy of the State" is. And if they like Uncle

Beau as much as I think they are going to like him, then maybe they'll see that as a way to acquit him!"

Dockett appeared stunned. "Well, your Judge Hixson is going to throw a fit, no doubt. But so long as he doesn't order me not to bring that out, I can't see the harm in it. And it certainly strengthens the point for the Circuit Court of Appeals. Like I said before, that's whom we're trying this case to."

Feeling more emboldened than before, Antonio responded, "Professor, I know that's what you've said. But there is a juror seated in the front row, juror #9. You won't be able to take your eyes off of her when you see her. Her name is Ana Katich. From the looks she has been giving me, I think she has been trying to tell me with her eyes: If I can find a way to get her the evidence, she will never convict Uncle Beau!"

Dockett gave Antonio an expression of surprise. "Hmm. Well, if you say so. It sounds to me like you're the one who can't keep your eyes off of her, but that's not such a bad thing! Jurors are funny, though. I can remember the time I tried a jury trial when I was a young man. There was this juror who kept nodding his head every time the prosecutor said anything. I thought my client was sunk. Then he was the foreperson, and the jury came back 'Not guilty.' I interviewed him later and asked why he voted not guilty, when he kept nodding at the prosecutor's remarks. You know what he told me?"

"What, Professor?"

"He said, 'I wasn't aware I was doing that. I just remember thinking how full of shit that prosecutor was! I must have been nodding, 'Yeah, there's another example!' And 'Yeah, there's another example!' And so on.' My point is, this Ana Katich may be trying to communicate a message to you, but it may not be the message you think she's communicating, and it may not be a message that you want to hear! Such as, 'you are such a good looking young man; what a shame I have to find your client guilty!' But regardless. So much of what goes into a jury trial comes down to intuition. If your intuition is that she's on your side, chances are pretty good that she is in fact on your side. And your idea plays the case to the Circuit Court of Appeals as well as to her! I say, do it! But let's go talk to your uncle, and make sure he understands our strategy!"

Antonio and Professor Dockett went to visit their client. They told Beau of their plan. But Antonio about fell over at his uncle's response:

"Don't want to testify."

"What?" Asked Professor Dockett. "Why?"

"Don't need to."

"Well," started in the professor, "If you mean that you don't think your testimony will add anything to the case, hmm, maybe so and maybe not. The issue is: Will it hurt you? It's been my experience that jurors want to hear from the accused, the Constitutional right not to testify notwithstanding. In a lot of cases, testifying is a really bad idea for the accused. I don't think yours is that case. As I understand it, you are a very well respected Congregational pastor who has quite a reputation in this community. I've heard nothing but great things from all of the people who love you."

Antonio chimed in. "Uncle Beau, he's right. This jury is going to love you. I can feel it. I know it. They are going to feel your softness. Your gentleness. Your honesty. Your morality. All you have to do, when the Professor asks you why you preached the Sermon on the Mount to the FBI, is that you were trying to get the FBI agents to understand that you are not an enemy of the State."

"That's what happened," replied Uncle Beau.

"Right!" said Antonio. "So, do you see? We're not asking you to say anything but the truth! If you just say that, my gut feeling is that this jury is going to acquit you, no matter what the jury instructions may say!"

Beau sat there for a very long time, saying nothing, but thinking. Dockett and Antonio wanted to interrupt the silence, but felt reluctance to do so. Finally, Beau said, "I'll testify."

Antonio and the Professor left the county jail. Antonio felt triumphant, that another idea of his would spring into reality, and it would work. But Dockett's response displayed a feeling of skepticism on the matter.

"You know," remarked the professor, "Your uncle is awfully quiet for a man of the cloth. He almost seems more like a 'Sioux Medicine Man' to me. Is he always that silent and that pithy?"

Antonio responded, "My momma has always told me how stoic he is, from the days when they both were children. And I think he's probably really nervous about this upcoming trial. And I think he's really scared. I mean, if you were looking at a life sentence, wouldn't you be really scared?"

Dockett replied, "Yes, but…"

Antonio interrupted, "I wouldn't worry. I've known my Uncle Beau my whole life. Outside of my momma, I can't think of anybody I love more than my Uncle Beau. He'll be full of a lot more adrenaline when the time comes, I'm sure of it. He'll do fine. And he's very smart, too. I can remember the debates he used to have with my grandmother. Grandma knew the Bible, but Uncle Beau knew it better, and he knew how to get his point across without insulting her, all while being absolutely right. Believe me, he'll make a great witness. That Atkinson won't put a dent in him. I know it!"

Dockett responded, "You know, I'm not so sure. Maybe your Uncle Beau has it right. Maybe he won't make the great witness that you think he will make. Quite frankly, your uncle's lack of verbal explanation in his answers bothers me. But on the other hand, how much about a person can you discern after a mere half hour of speaking with him or her? Like you've said, you have known your uncle your whole life. You know what Beau Browne is made of, and what makes him tick."

And thus the counsel agreed: Beau Browne was going on the witness stand.

XVIII

After Judge Hixson took his seat and introduced Professor Dockett to the jury, he instructed the defense team to call its first witness. Antonio called the leader of the Elders of the Congregational Church.

Q: Sir, let me show you Defense Exhibit One. Do you recognize it?

A: Yes.

Q: What is it?

A: It is a proclamation that the Elders of our Congregational Church wrote.

Q: When did they do this?

A: Two days after Pastor Browne was arrested and charged with Treason.

Q: What does it say?

A: It says: 'Consistent with and pursuant to Matthew 22:39 and Luke 10:25-37, the Congregational Church's charter is and shall be hereafter amended and clarified to state the following: All Pastors and everyone else preaching or giving spiritual aid will support the poor, the downtrodden, the homeless, and the hungry by all means necessary and appropriate, including taking such people into their abodes, feeding such people and finding employment for such people.'

Q: Did the Elders prepare this on the advice of Pastor Beau Browne's lawyers?

A: (laughing) We didn't prepare this on the advice of any lawyers! We didn't intend to codify the law! We intended to codify morality!

Q: Why did you do this?

At this point Atkinson objected, and cited the Fourth Circuit case and the Northern District of Texas case involving Bishop Monroe.

"Sustained," replied Hixson.

Once again, Antonio asked to be heard outside the presence of the jury. This time, the jury listened to the second movement of Tchaikovsky's *Pathetique Symphony* with choreographed images in their helmets of recruits marching at boot camp and chanting, "Sound off, one-two" in counterpoint to Tchaikovsky. Hixson instructed the jurors not to take off their virtual reality helmets, until the Court Services Officers tapped them on their shoulders.

"Your Honor," began Antonio, "If you will recall, you told Ms. Lopez when she was examining the Government's witness that this affirmative defense could not be proven through the Government. It had to be proven through a defense witness. That's what we are doing here."

"I understand that, young man," snapped Hixson. "The problem is that you are trying to establish your defense through a document that was prepared after your client harbored Mr. Kolkoski. It's meaningless."

"But it isn't, your Honor. Here is why: This witness is going to testify that the reason for this proclamation is to clarify what the charter of the Congregational Church has always meant. And it wasn't prepared at our request. The Elders prepared it on their own."

"Yes, counselor," said Hixson, again with "faux patience." "But they prepared it after the fact. It's irrelevant."

"Your Honor, I direct your attention to the SCOTUS opinions in *Fiore v. White* and *Bunkey v. Florida* from the early 21st century. The rule of law is plain: When interpreting a non-procedural statute, the interpretation by the court who is charged with interpreting the law applies retroactively, to the day the statute was passed into law, unless the interpretation is so novel that nobody could have foreseen it. Now, you would admit that Matthew 22:39 and Luke 10: 25-37 were around long before this church would you not?

Hixson responded, "Obviously. But that's the Bible!"

Quickly, Antonio responded: "Which is the law, the 'statute,' if you will, that governs this and all Christian churches, wouldn't you agree?"

Hixson was stopped in his tracks. Not only was this the first time in decades that he had felt like asking anything resembling a question of a lawyer, but also the lawyer's answers already had checkmated him. After a pause, Hixson continued,

"Are you trying to tell me that I should throw this case out on this basis?"

"No, I'm trying to tell you that you should allow this testimony in, uninterrupted, and you should then give a jury instruction at the close of the trial that says: 'If you find that the Charter of the Congregational Church has meant, since the Defendant's church was chartered, that its pastor may harbor someone – even an enemy of the State – if that is consistent with Matthew 22:39 and Luke 10: 25-37, then you must find the Defendant immune from prosecution and accordingly must find the Defendant not guilty.'"

Hixson responded with some horror: "Isn't that directing a verdict in favor of your client?"

Antonio knew the answer: "Not necessarily. If Mr. Atkinson can show the jury that harboring Mr. Kolkoski or the way he harbored Mr. Kolkoski was inconsistent with Matthew

22:39 and Luke 10:25-37, then the jury still could find the Defendant guilty."

Hixson was stunned. He hadn't thought of this, and on the surface it sounded awfully reasonable.

Trying to talk Antonio out of his idea, Hixson replied: "Well, it seems to me that a jury in this city naturally would agree with Mr. Atkinson in that regard."

Without missing a beat, Antonio had his reply: "Well, your Honor, we could certainly debate the point. But the rule of law has been plain for decades: The defense is entitled to any instruction on any recognized defense, no matter how weak or incredible the evidence in support of it may be, and no matter how many defenses he has."

Hixson hated admitting he was wrong. He hadn't done it in 45 years, but he came as close to admitting it now as he ever had:

"I will reverse myself, overrule the Government's objection, and allow this witness to finish his testimony. However, I'm going to think about how the jury instruction in question should really read. I'm not prepared to give it in the form you suggest, Mr. Lopez-Browne."

That may have been the biggest trial victory a criminal defense lawyer had ever obtained in the 45-year career of Jonah Hixson. Without missing a beat, Antonio continued his examination:

Q: Why did you prepare this Proclamation?

A: Because we wanted to clarify to all concerned, to all present and future Pastors, that this is what the Congregational Church has stood for since its inception. If someone like Adam Kolkoski had come to someone like Pastor Browne in 2048, for example, Pastor Browne's acts of kindness to Mr. Kolkoski would have been fully consistent with, authorized by, and directed by the charter of our church."

Antonio locked eyes with Ana Katich. He tried to send her this message: "Ms. Katich, remember how you promised me that if I could find a way for you to acquit the Defendant within the confines of the corrupt law, you would do it? You have just seen the divine loophole!"

Ana Katich gave Antonio Lopez-Browne a small smile, as if to say, "Message received."

But all that meant was the team of Dockett and Lopez-Browne had one juror on their side, at most. They needed another eleven. Pastor Browne needed to persuade those other eleven.

Fred Dockett called Pastor Browne to the stand. After going through his background and his credentials, the professor went straight to the relevant evidence:

Q: Pastor Browne, were you met by two agents of the FBI at your parsonage on January 23, 2051?

A: Yes.

Q: How did they enter your home?

A: With an army tank.

Q: Did they draw guns on you?

A: M-16A10's.

Q: Did they beat you?

Pastor Browne paused, and his eyes widened. Finally, A: Yes.

Q: Did they kick you?

His eyes widened some more. Finally, A: Yes.

Q: Did they shoot you with a Taser?

A: Yes.

Q: Did they water board you?

Again, Beau Browne didn't answer immediately, but ultimately, A: Later, yes.

Q: What did you say to the FBI?

A: I recited the Sermon on the Mount.

Q: How did they react?
A: They tried to drown me.
Q: What did you do in response?
A: I recited more of the Sermon on the Mount.
Q: Why did you do that? What message were you trying to send to the FBI?

Hixson saw where this was going, and came unglued from the bench. "Stop right there! Jury, put on your helmets, right now!" They did, and this time the music was the second movement of Beethoven's *Ninth Symphony* at 55 decibels with images of Army Rangers taking out the mid-twenty first century despot of Nigeria.

Hixson snarled at Dockett. "I see what you are trying to do! You've orchestrated a little ruse to have your client say that he isn't a terrorist, and Adam Kolkoski isn't an enemy of the State. I told your co-counsel, young Mr. Lopez-Browne here, earlier in this trial, that if he tried to pull that trick I'd hold him in contempt of court and he'd be spending the rest of this trial in jail! So you two tried to pretend that you, Dockett, didn't know anything about this and you, Dockett, decided to ask this line of questioning, figuring that you, Dockett, were immune from the County Jail! Well, guess what! You're not! You ask that question again, and you know where you're going!"

Hixson started to say something else, when suddenly there was a loud thud. Beau Browne had gone into what looked like a fit of some sort, maybe an epileptic fit, and the "thud" was the sound of him hitting the ground.

Everyone except the jury looked at Beau. The jury was too busy looking at the US Marine Air Corp, celebrating Christmas in Uzbekistan. The Court Services Officers helped Beau to his feet and got him some water. The jury continued to listen to the strains of Ludwig Van Beethoven only this time to *The Pastoral Symphony* with images of marines in their fatigues, coming home to the arms of their two-year-old daughters, with the jurors unaware of the commotion 100 feet in front of them. Once it appeared that Pastor Browne had regained his bearings, and was able to sit up again in the witness chair, Hixson had the Court Services Officers tap the jurors on their shoulders and remove their helmets. Hixson then looked at the lawyers and said, "Cross-examination!"

Dockett exploded. "I object!!"

"Jury, back with the helmets!" And the Court Services Officers had the jury put the helmets back on and put their heads down, this time listening to Bach's *Brandenburg Concerto* at about 60 decibels, while watching the opening clips from the old movie "Saving Private Ryan".

Dockett continued his explosion. "In the first place, I'm not done with my direct examination of this witness! In the second place, it is obvious what has just happened. I don't know if this witness is in any shape to testify! You could be subjecting my client to cruel and unusual punishment! This is outrageous!"

Hixson snarled at Dockett. "Counselor, are you trying to show contempt to this Honorable Court?"

"No, I'm trying to conceal it!"

Atkinson was horrified. Hixson's antics with Esperanza Lopez may have been worthy of a mistrial, and now it appeared inevitable that the masking tape would show its presence again. Chet thought fast:

"Objection, your Honor! My worthy opponent has just stolen that line from 'Rumpole of the Bailey'!"

That slowed Hixson down enough to keep the US Marshals from busting out the masking tape. Hixson smiled like a crocodile after a power lunch. "Sustained!"

That eased the tension, but only momentarily. After the jurors removed the helmets, the stubborn Hixson looked at Atkinson. "You may cross-examine."

Before Dockett could say anything, Atkinson put up his hand to stop him and said, "The Government has only one question to ask of Pastor Browne. And it is a simple 'yes or no' question. So, Pastor Browne, if you simply want just to nod your head, that's okay. The question is this: Pastor Browne, when you were telling Agents Gluck and Dombrowski the Sermon on the Mount, were you trying to convey the message to them that you do not believe yourself to be a terrorist and that, in your opinion, Adam Kolkoski is not an enemy of the State?"

As Beau nodded affirmatively and said, "Yes!" Hixson threw up his hands. "Counsel, approach the bench! Court recorder, turn off your video recorder!"

The lawyers approached. Hixson leaned over and hissed: "Mr. Atkinson, your former opponent, Ms. Lopez, seemed to accuse me of trying her case and losing it for her. You, sir, seem to be trying her case and winning it for her! What's the matter with you?!"

Atkinson looked at His Honor. "Your Honor, I object. You stole that line from the 1982 movie 'The Verdict'!"

This time, Hixson didn't crack a smile. Atkinson picked up the pieces from his bombed joke and, with royal irritation at Hixson, continued: "But otherwise, as I have said many times throughout this trial, the Government's position first and foremost is that this man receive a fair trial. I am trying like the devil to help you cure your errors! And notice how I phrased the question to the Defendant: I didn't say, 'Pastor Browne, were you trying to convey the message to the FBI that Kolkoski is not an enemy of the State'; I said, 'Pastor Browne, were you trying to convey *your opinion* to the FBI that Kolkoski is not an enemy of the State.' I can deal with his opinion in closing arguments. What I can't deal with is a defendant who passes out in front of the jury because the presiding judge has a hissy fit!"

If Hixson were truly an even-handed despot, he would have ordered Atkinson to spend the rest of the trial in jail. But he simply hissed, "All of you. Stand back."

But the antagonism between the judge and the lawyers had only just begun.

XIX

It came time for the settlement of jury instructions. Hixson took a brief recess while he crafted and put the instructions together. He then took the bench, gave the two lawyers the instructions, and said, "These are the instructions I propose to give. Speak now or forever hold your peace."

Antonio and Professor Dockett looked for the key First Amendment instruction, Instruction No. 13. They found it, and instantly felt horrified. It read:

"A defendant can be privileged to give aid to someone who is an enemy of the State, under certain circumstances. If you find that the Congregational Church charter means or meant, even before 2049, that a Congregational pastor may take into his home someone who later is determined to be an enemy of the State, you may find this Defendant not guilty.

However, a church cannot amend its charter after a Congregational pastor has already taken someone into his home."

"Your Honor," sputtered Dockett, "This instruction is unconstitutional. If you give it, a guilty verdict will certainly be reversed. You allowed the Congregational elder to testify, and now you are commenting on the evidence. You are telling the jury to give that evidence no weight. That is unconstitutional. Only a jury can decide what kind of weight to give to any evidence."

Hixson paused. It sounded like Dockett was probably right. He turned to Atkinson: "Government's position?"

Atkinson faced a key moment in this trial. A jury instruction like this probably would ensure a guilty verdict; and it probably would also ensure a reversal on appeal, for the reasons Dockett had stated. So the smooth Chet Atkinson responded:

"Your Honor, I think Professor Dockett is on to something. But here is how you get around that. Start your second paragraph with the words, "In the opinion of this Court," and end the paragraph with "You are not bound by this opinion."

Dockett responded, "Nice try. But a judge doesn't give a jury 'opinions'; he gives them the governing law. The instruction as Mr. Atkinson has phrased it is another way of saying, 'Pay no attention to the purple rhinoceros in your living room'! I object. I say just take the whole second paragraph out."

"No," responded Hixson. "I'm not going to do that. But I am going to follow Mr. Atkinson's suggestion, and put in the opinion language into the jury instruction."

Dockett and Antonio may not have appreciated that this was the first time in 45 years that the defense, with the aid of the prosecution, had ever convinced Judge Hixson to change his mind and amend a jury instruction on anything. But the victory was small. The instruction gave both sides what they wanted for argument purposes, but ultimately it was going to depend on how much weight the jury was going to give to Judge Hixson's opinion. And generally, juries tend to give a lot of weight to the trial judge's opinion, no matter how big an idiot the trial judge happens to be.

Atkinson led off, and everyone in the courtroom felt surprise by the monotone in his voice, and the abruptness of his speech. His opening salvo went like this:

"Ladies and gentlemen: The facts are not in dispute, and neither is the law. Beau Ezekiel Browne harbored someone who is an enemy of the State. That's the beginning, the end, and the bottom line. Based on that, you must find him guilty.

The only thing to talk about is what is covered in Instruction no. 13. Now, the judge just read that to you. And the defense called the Elder of the Congregational Church to talk about that proclamation. The problem is that the Elders created that proclamation after the fact. Of course they wanted to help their pastor, their friend, Pastor Beau Browne. And you can understand why. But to make up a proclamation after the fact? If that's what the Congregational Church charter meant from the very beginning, why didn't the Church just say so from the outset?"

Atkinson wanted to read from the instruction, and emphasize what Judge Hixson's opinion was. But he stopped himself. He thought: *If I do that, and if the Court of Appeals holds that this instruction is erroneous, they will reverse the conviction because I have emphasized it.*

So, Atkinson continued: "Therefore, use your common sense. Look, how long have poor and oppressed people been around? Since the dawn of mankind. And how long have convicted sex offenders who are subject to community notification requirements been around? For decades. There have been a lot of people that Congregational Church pastors nationwide could have harbored. But they didn't. And for good reason. You don't know that much about people at the end of the day. You don't know what's in their hearts. Yes, I agree that there may be someone who suffers a felony conviction and who later completely reforms. But I also submit to you that there are people who suffer felony convictions and, even years later, would steal anything from your house that wasn't bolted down, given half a chance. So, you have to be careful. And Pastor Beau

Browne wasn't careful. Does that make him a bad man? No, believe it or not, I don't think it does. But we live in terrible times. There are plenty of bad people out there. If we as a nation are going to survive, we have to be careful. That's why we have The Super Patriot Act of 2049, to force us to be careful. It's the law, and we are bound to follow it. For that reason, you must find Pastor Beau Browne guilty. That is your duty under the law."

Fred Dockett ambled up to the podium. He knew he was going to have to give the closing argument of his illustrious career to overcome Atkinson's opening closing argument. Dockett cleared his throat, and then spoke:

"Ladies and gentlemen, when you go into the jury room, you will do your duty, as Mr. Atkinson suggests. And in doing your duty, you are going to fill out and sign off on the Not Guilty verdict form. Let me tell you why you are going to do that:

Think back to the evidence given on the first day of the trial. The Government says that my client harbored an enemy of the State. How did they prove that? Well, they had a sex offender registry card, which said a Mr. Kolkoski lived at the address that happens to be Pastor Browne's parsonage. But you heard the FBI's Special Agent's testimony: A lot of times sex offenders will give false information to the local police. So the fact that an Adam Kolkoski filled out a card -- and by the way, they didn't have to, but wouldn't it have been nice if the Government could have produced Mr. Kolkoski on the witness stand? -- Doesn't prove anything other than one simple fact: Someone bearing a signature of an Adam Kolkoski filled out this card. That's the best we can say about that.

It would have been very simple for Agent Gluck or Agent Dombrowski, once they entered the parsonage, to look around for evidence of Kolkoski's residence. A quick glance in the spare bedroom for clothes hanging in the closet, or toiletries on the bathroom vanity, or an unmade bed, for example. But they didn't do that. They weren't interested in doing that. They were interested in doing one and only one thing: torturing a man of the cloth. That's why they are known as 'Agent Gloom' and 'Agent Doom'. That's what they do. That's what they enjoy doing.

You saw Agent Gluck's attitude from the witness stand. He described the torture process like he was cooking yesterday's breakfast. 'A little tasing here, add a kick to the head there, with a punch to the solar plexus over here and a rifle whip to the face of a kind, gentle man over yonder, and voilá: We have a soufflé of shock and awe.' The fact that this kind, gentle man begged them to stop just gave Gloom and Doom more energy to keep on torturing Pastor Browne.

You have a jury instruction that tells you that if you find a confession is involuntarily given, you may disregard the entirety of it. And I would submit to you that the moral response to this case, certainly the correct response to this case, is to disregard every single thing that Pastor Browne said to Gluck and Dombrowski.

Why? Because from the very beginning, Gluck and Dombrowski came in with an Army tank, M-16A10s, paramilitary uniforms and combat helmets. To a Congregational pastor's home? Really? What's that all about? How is that even necessary? Whatever happened to the days where you knocked on the front door, respected a man's home as his castle, and acted civilized? Have we really come to the point in this country where the only way the police can investigate crime is to go into what I call a 'shock and awe' military mode? Even when it's the parsonage of a Congregational pastor's home? Has law enforcement lost its collective mind?

Now, you know my answer to that, but my answer doesn't matter. It's your answer that matters. And let me let you in on a little secret, ladies and gentlemen. The Government apparently thinks it is perfectly fine to treat a kind, gentle man in this fashion. But they are not the Government any more. You are. You. Yes, you. Each and every one of the twelve of you. And each of you has the ability to look the FBI and the DOJ right in their two eyes and say, 'If you are going to treat our citizens like this, if you are going to torture them like this in order to try to get information, then we are not going to pay attention to anything they say to you. And if you otherwise are too lazy to try to figure out the suspected crime, then you don't get your conviction. If you're that lazy, then you haven't proven the suspected crime beyond a reasonable doubt. Next time try harder. If treason charges are really that important to you, then try harder.'

I urge you to go into that jury room with that kind of fortitude, with that kind of resolve. And if you do, maybe just maybe the Government will stop 'torturing folks' as a way of getting their convictions. I for one would welcome that change of thinking in Washington."

In retrospect, we simply cannot know how the jury would have voted if Dockett had stopped right there. Give Esperanza Lopez credit for one thing: Under the circumstances, if she had said those words, she probably would have finished the argument and sat down. With Jury Instruction No. 13, she would have realized she didn't have a First Amendment defense to work with any longer, and putting the FBI on trial for torture was the only realistic thing she could talk about and make an issue of. But Dockett believed that "throwing everything against the wall, and hoping something might stick, at least for the Circuit Court of Appeals," was the way to approach and to advocate this case. And thus he went on:

"And since you are now the Government, not Mr. Atkinson, not Judge Hixson, but you, consider something else:

You heard the testimony of the head Elder of the Congregational Church. You have the proclamation in evidence. As far as that church is concerned, giving aid to the needy, the unfortunate, the downtrodden, has been the word of the Lord ever since the Bible was written. The Bible wasn't written in 2051, or in 2049. It was written, as you know, centuries and centuries before that. Jesus Christ told his people, in the greatest commandment of all and in the parable of the Good Samaritan, what we do with people like Adam Kolkoski. When they become jobless, and become homeless, we take them in. We give them comfort. If necessary, we give them shelter. We give them food.

Isn't it unfortunate, indeed, isn't it damning to America, that things have come to this? That a church has to legislate some common sense into the people because Congress won't do it for us? Isn't that a sad state of affairs?"

Immediately, Atkinson objected. Immediately, Hixson sustained the objection. "Counselor," admonished Hixson, "move on to something else, now!"

Dockett acted nonplussed. Without asking for a sidebar conference and in front of the jury, Dockett said, "I don't understand, your Honor. What did I say that was so wrong?"

Hixson hissed at him. "You were about to tell the jury to do what I told you I'd throw you in jail for if you did it!"

The next question sounded dumb, but coming from Dockett, it was calculated to be anything but dumb. "I don't understand. What was I about to tell the jury that could land me in jail?"

Hixson, without thinking about what he was saying, or talking outside the presence of the jury, replied, "You were about to tell the jury that they can ignore the law and acquit someone because the law is wrong!"

Dockett's next question well proved that he had planned something ingenuous wrapped in a simpleton's clothing. In a nonplussed tone of voice, Dockett asked, "So, you meant to say that a jury could ignore the law and acquit someone because the law is wrong?"

Hixson first said, "Yes," then immediately he shouted, "No! You know the answer is 'no'! The jury is never allowed to do that!"

Now it is time for some petard-hoisting, thought Rocket Dockett. "But that is just your opinion, and you said in your jury instruction that the jury isn't bound by your opinion, is that correct?"

Hixson shrilly cried at Dockett: "Yes. No, wait! No, that's not correct, and you know it! Your 'First Amendment immunity' defense and your 'enemy of the State' defense are two different defenses, and you know it!"

Dockett was at an advantage because he had thought it through. Slowly and thoughtfully, he said, "So that I understand what I can argue to the jury, your Honor: Let's say a member of the Taliban comes to America, with the clear intent to overthrow the American government. But while detonating a bomb he severely injures his leg. Let's suppose further that the charter of the nearby church specifically allows the minister, priest or rabbi to take the Taliban member into his parsonage to give him shelter, aid and comfort, consistent with the teachings of Christianity, Buddhism or Judaism. Do I understand that in that instance, the Taliban is clearly an enemy of the State, but the minister, priest or rabbi is clearly immune from prosecution?"

Judge Hixson didn't realize that Dockett had just "checkmated" him. If Hixson were to say "no, that's not right," then Hixson would be playing right into Dockett's hand, that the two defenses were mirror images of the same defense, and the jury would know that it was not bound by Hixson's "opinion" regarding the law. So, Hixson said, "That is correct, counselor."

"So, the state of the law in the United States of America is this: If a member of the Taliban who clearly intends to overthrow the US Government injures himself in the process, and a man of the cloth takes him into his home because the charter of his church, temple or synagogue specifically allows him to do so, that man is immune from prosecution. But if an unsuspecting US citizen who was ensnared in a government-manufactured sex sting and hasn't gotten into any trouble for 45 years since then finds himself practically suicidal because of what society has done to him, a man of the cloth may not take him into his home and give him comfort, unless the charter of his church, at the very time that man is practically suicidal, specifically allows him to do so? That is your opinion on the state of the law?"

The courtroom's silence struck even the most casual observer. Dockett had checkmated Hixson, and the crotchety old judge knew it. How would he respond?

Like he always did, of course. "You're in contempt of court, counselor! But rather than go to jail, I will simply strike your entire argument, and turn this case over to the jury right now! And if you object, I will do all of that and send you to jail for the rest of this trial!"

And immediately, Atkinson thought, *Oh, for God's sake, Hixson! Here, I keep trying to save this case from yourself, and you keep blowing it! If you strike Dockett's entire argument for that reason, I don't care on appeal which three judges on the Circuit hear this case. Any panel of three judges is going to reverse this. You're making my job way harder than it needs to be!*

Atkinson spoke. "Your Honor, may I suggest something before the jury is handed the case?"

Hixson glared, "What now?"

"Don't hold Mr. Dockett in contempt and don't strike his argument. Let me handle it in the Government's rebuttal closing argument."

Hixson was still furious. Dockett had caused Hixson to ring the bell and Hixson knew he couldn't unring it. If Atkinson thought he could do so, then great. He didn't want to change his mind on the contempt citation, but it was more important for the Government to obtain its conviction.

"So ordered. Go ahead, Mr. Atkinson."

Atkinson got up and said, "Ladies and gentlemen," but he was looking straight at Ana Katich as he spoke. "Don't misunderstand me. In my opinion, torture is a terrible thing, and my client was wrong to torture Pastor Browne. Believe me, somebody back in Washington, D.C. is going to be upset with me for saying that, but I said it and I'm glad I did. But if you want to ignore what Pastor Browne said while he was being tortured, you then must ignore the Sermon on the Mount. And if you ignore that, then you ignore religion and the religious angle to this case altogether!

Instead, you focus on what happened before Gloom and Doom dunked Pastor Browne into the Terrorist Baptismal Tank. And when you focus on that, you realize that Pastor Browne confessed to harboring Adam Kolkoski. And Adam Kolkoski is an enemy of the State, as the Department of Justice has defined the term and as your jury instructions have defined the term.

Now, Mr. Dockett has suggested to you that you should also ignore Pastor Browne's confession because the FBI knocked down his front door with an army tank and appeared with military rifles, wearing paratrooper gear. But what

Professor Dockett overlooks is that every police agency in this country, from Adelanto to Zanesville, has been doing that in this country for 50 years now! And in this case, if the police think that someone is harboring a terrorist in their home, they have every right to enter the home in that fashion. They don't have to knock. They don't have to give the homeowner the opportunity to open the door. And the fact that the home in this case is the parsonage of a Congregational pastor is irrelevant. Call it an inconvenient truth, if you will; but it's irrelevant. In the US, no matter who you are, if you are suspected of harboring an enemy of the State, the price you pay for doing so is to have the front door of your home mowed down by a tank. That's just the way it is. Call it an obligation of citizenship, if you will. So, if you are going to do that, you forfeit your right to claim that you are a victim of torture, until you are actually tortured.

For that reason, like it or not, Pastor Beau Browne is guilty and you must find him so. Thank you for your close attention to this most difficult case, ladies and gentlemen."

The jury deliberated for 13 hours. As much as Atkinson, Lopez-Browne and Dockett wanted to leave the federal courthouse and hang out at the nearby bar or café, they simply couldn't do that. Even so, Atkinson and Dockett started a conversation while seated on the hard walnut benches outside the courtroom. Antonio said nothing, but listened intently while the two master craftsmen spoke:

"Professor," said Atkinson, "I have to tell you, what you did to Hixson was just one of the greatest jobs of tying a judge into knots I've ever seen. I think you won the case with that tactic!"

"Funny you should say that," replied Dockett. "I thought your final closing argument, and the way you caused Hixson to let you make it, was nothing short of brilliant. I think you snatched victory from the jaws of defeat with that one!"

Immediately the lawyers were hailed into court. Hixson said, "We have a question from the jury. It says: 'If we follow the law in this case, will we be condemned to hell?'"

With a twinkle in his eye, Dockett responded, "Your Honor, the correct answer to that question is 'yes.'"

Hixson snarled at him. "Mr. Dockett, don't push your luck with me. The answer I'm giving the jury is 'Refer back to your jury instructions and no other instructions.'"

Back outside the courtroom, Atkinson said to Dockett, "Well, with a question like that, I think the jury has figured out its ability to be lawless. I think the score of this ballgame is 'Browne 1, the US Government 0.'"

Dockett replied, "I'm not so sure."

A few hours later, the attorneys again were hailed into the courtroom. Judge Hixson said, "We have another question from the jury: 'If torture is morally wrong, why does it matter whether the Defendant confessed before the torture began or afterwards?' Gentlemen?"

Dockett responded, "I'm not sure a lawyer or a judge could answer that question; but I believe an ethicist could. I suppose you could give them a 'tortuous' response!"

Hixson did not laugh; in fact, he may not have understood the joke. "I'm responding that they will have to refer back to the jury instructions given and no other instruction."

The two trial lawyers went outside on the same benches by the courtroom, and renewed their conversation, while Antonio continued to listen intently:

"You know," said Atkinson, "I've been a DOJ lawyer my entire career, but cases like this really cause me to lose sleep at night. I view myself as a good soldier who just does what the DOJ tells me to do, and almost always I feel good about bringing bad guys to justice. But not in this case. I don't know that I've ever seen a case where I've rooted for the other side as much as this one."

Dockett replied, "My advice to you is simple, Chet: When things get to that point in your job, resign. You know, the last law firm I was in before I went to Cornell had a managing partner who was a maniac. He wanted eight billable hours a day out of every lawyer in that firm."

"You're kidding!' Atkinson responded. "How could any lawyer do that legitimately?"

Dockett replied, "To do that legitimately, you'd have to work at least 60 hours a week, whether the workload justified that kind of billing schedule or not."

"Yeah, and never get sick or have an off day!" Atkinson laughed.

"Yeah, exactly," said Dockett. "Meaning, I literally lost sleep at night. And after a few years of that kind of grinding, I realized a major truth: Resignation was the only sensible option. If somebody else wants to work him or herself into an early heart attack, all in the name of chasing the almighty dollar, that is his or her prerogative. Just keep me out of it!"

Atkinson smiled. "You know, I'd love to have a drink with you, but right now doesn't look like the time. But any time you're in DC, or any time I'm in upstate New York, let's get together!"

Dockett shook Atkinson's hand. "You know what? I'd like that! Win or lose, it's been a pleasure. You and I are complete professionals, and I think it's a good idea to surround yourself with complete professionals!"

In time, the Court Services Officers hailed the lawyers into court again. Judge Hixson said, "The jury has another question: 'Why should a Christian church feel it's necessary to amend its charter at all?'"

Dockett said, "I could guess which juror asked that one, and it's a damned good question. It's why I think the Fourth Circuit is wrong as hell. Maybe that juror needs to get a law degree and move to Virginia!"

Judge Hixson snarled, "No need to debate this one. I'm referring them to the previous jury instructions and no other instructions."

The lawyers went back outside the courtroom, and were about to exchange more professional pleasantries, when they heard a noise. With the hard marble floors and the high ceilings throughout that floor of the courtroom, the noise became amplified. They went toward the jury deliberation room, and could hear screaming. "My God," said Atkinson, "Is somebody going to kill someone in there? Better start handing out your business cards, Fred!" They laughed.

One hour later, the Clerk announced: The jury had reached a verdict.

When the Clerk stated, "All rise for the jury," the three lawyers looked at the jury. Dockett knew instantly that he had just lost his second case in a year. Ana Katich had red eyes and running makeup. None of the twelve would look at Beau Browne, much less smile at him.

"Will the Clerk please read the verdict," said Hixson.

"We, the jury, upon our oath do say, that we find the defendant, Beau Ezekiel Browne, guilty of the charge of treason. Dated this 21st day of December, 2051."

Hixson polled the jury. "Is this your true and correct verdict?"

The first eight jurors simply said, "Yes." But Juror #9, Ana Katich, said, "It is my true verdict. It is not a correct verdict, however."

"What?" Asked Judge Hixson, in an intimidating tone. "Are you telling this Court that you wish to go back into the jury room and change your vote?"

"No, that's not what I mean," replied Ana Katich. "I have no desire to see that room, ever again. I am telling you that I have agreed to the 'Guilty' verdict. But I am also telling you that the jury as a whole has reached the wrong result with the 'Guilty' verdict, in my opinion."

However Dockett and Atkinson may have felt while walking out of the federal building, Antonio felt like he just got whacked in the back of his head with a spike-filled two-by-four. His Uncle Beau, the man he loved more than any other man in his life, now would spend the rest of his life in prison. And this happened on Antonio's watch. Antonio started to sob.

As Antonio headed for his car behind the federal building, choking, with his head down, a sudden, loud noise caused him to look up. The 12 jurors headed off the back elevator that led to the back part of the building, near the front row of that lot. And Antonio heard Ana Katich scream and point at the other 11 jurors:

"You were wrong! You were wrong! You know you were wrong! You will have to live with yourselves, knowing you were wrong! When you die, God will meet you in heaven, and the first thing He will say to you is, 'you were wrong! You should have listened to Ana Katich from Serbia!"

Antonio knew he had to follow up on this. Could this be a case of jury misconduct? Could Uncle Beau win a new trial based on jury misconduct?

Antonio called her up, nervously. He really wanted to meet Ana Katich and to know more about her, but not like this, necessarily.

"I was so hoping you would call me, Mr. Lopez-Browne."

"Please, call me Antonio."

Ana paused, and much later told Antonio her thought: *Already this conversation is off to a good start!*

"Antonio, I feel so badly about what happened. I feel like I let you down."

Part of Antonio wanted to say, "You did." But a bigger part wanted to say, and did say, the following:

"I thought from the looks that you gave me throughout the trial that you were going to vote to acquit my Uncle Beau. But..."

"No, I did," Ana interrupted. "The jury was first hung, 6-6. Then, 7-5 for conviction. Then 9-3. Then 11-1. I voted to acquit each time...hold on, did you say your Uncle Beau?"

"Yes. I am Antonio Lopez-Browne. My mother is Bonita Browne. Her brother is Beau Browne."

"And your mother is.... Oh, my God! Esperanza Lopez!"

"Yes. She is my mother. Bonita Browne actually is my Momma."

Ana started to laugh a musical laugh, then stopped. "Oh, I'm so sorry to laugh. This must have been so hard for you. You had to see your mother humiliated by that awful judge, and then we found your uncle guilty."

"Not only found guilty, but now he is serving the rest of his life in prison on account of the guilty verdict."

Ana Katich said nothing.

"Ms. Katich, Ms. Katich, are you still there? Ms. Katich?"

Antonio then heard a soft sound of crying.

"Ms. Katich, what's the matter?"

"Oh, God, I feel so terrible. You see, I was the one who posed all of those questions to the judge when we were deciding the verdict. I was hoping the judge would answer them in such a way that the other jurors would see the error of their thinking. But the judge would not answer them. And the others, they kept siding with the prosecutor. I refused to find your uncle guilty. Then they ganged up on me. They bullied me. They wanted to go home. They called me names. They called me a 'bimbo.' They said I was young and naïve, and didn't understand the ways of the country. That just made me madder, and more determined not to find your uncle guilty. Then I remembered what I said during jury selection: I said if the law is corrupt, I must follow the law because it has been pre-ordained. I realized I said that, and I am a woman of my word. I had to find your uncle guilty. But in my mind, the way I made it all right with myself is, I thought that under the circumstances, the judge would give your uncle probation, or maybe a year in jail. I had no idea that what he did meant a life sentence! And I know the other jurors did not know that, either."

Antonio said, "That was on purpose. By law, the jury isn't supposed to know what the sentencing consequence of a guilty verdict is."

Ana responded, "That is a stupid law."

Antonio replied: "You know what? I agree with you! In a civil case, the jury not only decides liability, they decide how much in damages to award if the defendant is liable. So, the jurors not only know the consequences of their decision in a civil case, they decide those consequences. But they don't do that in a criminal case, except in first-degree murder cases. I think if jurors knew what the sentencing consequences of their guilty verdicts were, you wouldn't see quite so many guilty verdicts in this country."

Ana said, "Now that I know that, if I had a chance to go back into that jury room, I never would have voted to convict your uncle. As I think back on it, yes, I did say that if the law is corrupt, I must follow it because it is preordained that the American Empire will fall because of corrupt law. But when I heard the evidence of how the FBI tortured your uncle, I changed my mind."

Antonio asked, "What made you change your mind?"

And Ana spoke what she had envisioned when she heard Gluck's testimony. "You see, my family was persecuted in Serbia for generations. The Ustase at the Jasenovac Concentration Camp following World War II tortured my great-grandfather. The Croats tortured my grandfather during the great Yugoslavian Civil War of the 1990's. I came to America, angry with your government for not stopping the Croats when they should have, but secure in knowing that here, I would never be tortured. When I heard that evidence about what the FBI did to your uncle, I knew that my security now was in jeopardy. I knew that if the FBI could torture your uncle, they could torture anybody. And I realized that to shrug my shoulders at this corrupt law would be like my great-grandfather shrugging his shoulders at Jasenovac. But with the eleven jurors pressuring me, I did not stand up and say what was in my heart. I let them bully me. If there was only some way I could take it back...."

Antonio Lopez-Browne said the next words on instinct. This was the most instinctual thing he had ever said in his very planned life:

"Ms. Katich,"

Ana interrupted Antonio. "Please, Antonio, call me Ana."

"Of course. Ana, would you have coffee with me so that we can talk about what we might do about this?"

"No."

Antonio was crushed. *Of course she'd say 'no.' Here I am, the world's biggest nerd. I've been a loner all my life. No beautiful girl has ever said 'yes' to me before. But I've never asked a beautiful girl to say 'yes' to me before. I don't know how to ask. I'm 32 years old, and I don't know how to ask. So, why on earth would the world's most beautiful, most intelligent, most perfect woman ever say 'yes' to me? Why did I set the bar so high?*

And then Ana said, "But I will have dinner with you."

On instinct, Antonio said, "What kind of restaurant would you like?"

"In this town, buffet."

They met that evening at the nicest buffet in the nicest, five-star hotel in town. In the meantime, Antonio researched the law, and told Ana the bad news:

"As much as I would love to have you sign an affidavit on what happened, the judge would strike it."

Ana replied, "Of course he would. That judge was awful. If he sat with a bare bottom on a hot stove and screamed, I would not believe him!"

Antonio laughed. He had never heard that expression before. Ana Katich was so charming, so captivating, that Antonio forgot to give her his legal lecture on how and why a juror can't nullify her own verdict, based purely on what happens in the jury deliberation room. What the other 11 jurors did to make Ana change her mind and vote "guilty" was perfectly legal. Nasty and cruel, maybe, but legal. But Ana Katich did not give off signals that she was the slightest bit interested in hearing a legal lecture, and fortunately for Antonio, on this evening he did not misread her.

That evening, Antonio Lopez-Browne and Ana Katich did not solve the problems of the Super Patriot Act of 2049 or of the guilty verdict of Beau Ezekiel Browne. But when it came to leaving the tip for the waiter, they addressed another particular issue. Antonio had paid at the cashier's station for the two dinners. Ana went to her purse to leave the tip. When she put the $5 bill on the table, Antonio stopped her, pressing her hand. She turned her wrist slightly, and grabbed his hand, dropping the money.

The electricity from their touch in both of them surged through Ana and Antonio's bodies. Both felt like they had just added 500 watts to the restaurant's bank of lighting.

Before long, they stood up, still holding each other's hand, then held each other. Then they kissed. No awkward neck bending; they went to each other's lips instantly. To Antonio, Ana's lips felt and tasted like the ripest, sweetest cherry he had ever tasted. They could not stop holding and kissing each other. To Antonio and Ana nothing around them mattered. Their souls were too busy, kissing and enveloping each other. They both realized in that moment: They had finally found their soul mates.

From that day forward, Antonio and Ana were inseparable. Antonio had made love to a woman in his life before, to a couple of coeds in college who had each thrown themselves at Antonio. But those young women didn't even begin to compare with Ana. On Antonio's first attempt at lovemaking, Ana sensed his nervousness, but guided him through the lovemaking process like an old pro. And after the first time they made love, they could not keep their hands and their lips off of each other. Each hungered for each other daily. And the happiest for the couple of all was Bonita Browne. Bonita felt like she finally had the daughter she always had wanted, and was the happiest she had been in 30 years.

One day in the winter of 2052 Ana confronted Antonio:

"Antonio: I love your momma. She is so nice, so sweet. But I haven't met your mother yet. Don't you think I should?"

Antonio did not look at his girlfriend. Instead he dropped his head and with a dark look said, "You never will. We don't speak."

Ana said with some alarm: "But it won't always be that way, will it?"

Finally, after slowly turning his head toward Ana, Antonio said this: "Do you remember her from the trial?"

Ana laughed. "I don't think anyone who sat through that trial could soon forget her!"

Antonio bluntly and with finality replied: "You saw all you need to know."

One month later, while walking together in the city square around the patches of melting snow, Antonio Lopez-Browne asked Ana Katich for her hand in marriage. Ana stopped, looked at Antonio, and replied, "Yes, on one condition."

"Name it."

"I will not change my name. From now until the day I die, I am Ana Katich from Serbia."

And Antonio replied, "In that case, I will change mine. From now until the day I die, I am Antonio Browne-Katich."

"Isn't that disrespectful to your mother?"

Antonio took his bride-to-be's hands into his, looked deep into her soulful eyes, and said this:

"My last name should reflect the two most important people in my life. That would be Bonita Browne and Ana Katich. I don't know how badly my mother will be hurt by my decision. But I don't care. She bullied me my whole life. Then she abandoned me when I needed her. Someday she will realize the damage she has done to me."

"Do you really believe that?" asked Ana.

"I really do. And when she does, she will learn to get over her hurt."

And Ana simply replied: "And when she does, I will be there for you."

XXI

Christmas season of 2051 defined lives, not only for Beau, Ana and Antonio, but also for Bonita and Esperanza.

Bonita went on Christmas Eve to the Assembly of God, where she had been a parishioner for the past 40 years. As she sat in her familiar pew and finished singing the first hymn, she felt a hand on her shoulder. She turned around, and there she saw Esperanza, standing behind her.

When Antonio dropped Bonita off at the battered woman's shelter, the administrator told her that as a condition of staying there, the shelter recommended that she seek to have Esperanza arrested for domestic battery, but Bonita absolutely had to get a domestic violence restraining order against Esperanza. And if Bonita would not have Esperanza arrested for domestic battery, Bonita had to have the restraining order extended, such that Esperanza must stay away from her for three years. And, in order to stay in the shelter, she – not only Esperanza, but also Bonita – had to abide by the Order. That meant both Esperanza and Bonita knew Esperanza could not have any contact with Bonita at least until late 2054.

Bonita screamed, "Get out of here! You're not supposed to be here!"

Esperanza interrupted, "No, I need to talk to you!"

"Get out of here! Go away! Leave!"

"Come on, Bo! It's Christmas!"

"No! You get out! I'm going to call the cops!!"

"In this church? Quit being ridiculous, Bo! Just talk to me, will you?"

"No! You can't be here! No!"

This scene stopped the Christmas Eve service. The minister understandably expressed irritation. "Ushers, remove these two from the service, now!"

The ushers knew Bonita quite well, well enough to understand the situation. When Esperanza left their sight, the usher holding Bonita's arm walked her from the church's parking lot back to the church's narthex and said, "Call 911 right now."

"Why?"

"Don't ask why. Just do it."

Within five minutes the police arrived. And upon hearing the story they arrested Esperanza Lopez on Christmas Eve, in the Assembly of God parking lot, and took her to jail on charges of violating the domestic violence restraining order.

Esperanza spent twelve hours, late Christmas Eve to mid Christmas day, in the overcrowded county jail, seated in the "drunk tank" with some grossly intoxicated Christmas celebrants. All of the humiliation Judge Jonah Hixson had bestowed upon Esperanza Lopez during the Beau Browne trial paled in comparison with the humiliation she felt in the county jail on Christmas Eve. She found herself about as far removed from "peace on earth, good will toward men" as possible.

Esperanza appeared three days after Christmas before the municipal court judge. By that point the arresting officer had written his declaration of probable cause to arrest, and the judge read it before taking the bench in the tiny courtroom.

"Ms. Lopez, how do you plead?"

"I am innocent! I had the absolute right under the First Amendment to be in the church of my choice!"

The judge, a kindly old soul, was a lawyer serving as a temporary (*pro tem*) judge while the regularly seated judge enjoyed his vacation. "No, no, Ms. Lopez. I didn't ask you whether you were innocent. I asked you, how do you plead?"

Esperanza replied with defiance, "If I am absolutely privileged under the First Amendment to do what I did, I shouldn't have to plead in front of you at all. I stand mute!"

The judge, a wise, middle-aged man, knew who Esperanza Lopez was. He knew of her reputation, and had heard what happened to her during the Beau Browne trial. He also knew that Esperanza had already written the judicial discipline complaint in her head, or the complaint to that court to remove him from the *pro tem* list, before he had said anything. But then, he had a brainstorm on the spot:

"Ms. Lopez, let me do something a little bit unorthodox, and ask you a few questions, if I may. As I understand the situation, you were served with an extended domestic violence restraining order, ordering you to stay away from Bonita Browne for three years. Am I right?"

"That's true, your Honor. And I..."

The judge cut her off. "Hold it, hold it. Stop, please. And as I further understand the situation, you think that you were absolutely privileged to violate the order because you did so inside the four walls of a church. Is that correct."

"Finally, you get it."

"Well, before I agree with you that I've 'got it' completely, let me ask you this: While you were in the Assembly of God, did you pray?"

"No, but I was about to."

"Did you sing a hymn?"

"No, but I intended to."

"Did you ask for Bonita Browne's forgiveness, or better yet, declare your forgiveness of Bonita Browne?"

"That's just it, your Honor. I went there to do all of that, and she wouldn't let me say what was on my mind."

"So, your answer is 'no.' 'No, but' or 'No, because' still means 'No.' I'm sure you've told that to witnesses many times in depositions you've conducted. True?"

Esperanza saw where the conversation might be going, and said, "True, but this…"

The judge put up his hand. "Stop, stop, stop, Ms. Lopez. Please, stop. 'True, but' also means 'True.' Listen carefully to me, please.

I'm a pro tem judge who ordinarily practices law. That means today is the only day you and I will cross paths on this case. Okay? It seems to me that you have a choice. You have two options. The first one is to plead Not Guilty; or if you prefer to stand mute, I will enter a 'Not Guilty' plea for you. If you do that, we'll set your trial date. All right? But you will not get a jury trial. You will get a bench trial before Judge Woo. Do you understand? I have to tell you, I'm normally a lot more tolerant and understanding than Judge Woo is. I can't speak for Judge Woo, of course. But your First Amendment defense hasn't impressed me in the least. Of course, it could impress Judge Woo. But my prediction is that he will act even more negatively towards it than I have. Do you see what I'm saying?

But if you want to take that option, you certainly may. It's up to you. Okay? Of course, I should add, knowing Judge Woo as I do, my educated guess is that he not only will reject your First Amendment defense, he will sentence you to some time in jail. He has to, you see? The legislature won't let him get away with a mere fine. I mean, he could order you to do community service, or even allow you to serve your time on house arrest; but knowing Judge Woo as I do, I predict a month of jail for you. And you can appeal his decision if you want to. All right? But you will serve your entire sentence in jail, before the appellate decision comes out. He typically doesn't grant bail pending appeal from his decisions. Just so you know. Do you understand me?

The second option that you have – and again, it's up to you, okay? -- Is this: You can plead no contest to me right now. I will accept your no contest plea, but I will not enter a judgment. I will order you to go to bi-weekly domestic violence counseling, at your expense, for the next six months. Got it? If you show up to all of the counseling sessions and participate, and show some progress, at the end of six months the court will set aside your no contest plea and dismiss the charges. All right? And I'll order that the record of your arrest be sealed at that point. You will have gained the result you hoped to gain from the First Amendment, and then some. Of course, if you contact Ms. Browne again, Judge Woo will enter a formal judgment, he can send you to jail for up to six months and fine you $1,000, and you won't really have the right to appeal. But it's your choice, Ms. Lopez. What do you want to do?"

Esperanza Lopez stood there. She knew she couldn't file a complaint against this guy. The judicial discipline commission had no jurisdiction over a *pro tem* judge. And he was a kind man who said what he said in a kind way. And he gave her a choice. He hadn't ordered her to do anything. And then, the enormity of the moment finally, finally hit her.

She was a shit. Not "the shit"; "a shit." Just a free-floating turd in the septic tank of life. She had been a shit for at least forty years. Her life? Shit. All of her money, all of her art, all of her trips to Jamaica and the Bahamas, all of her reputation, all of her million-dollar settlements, all of the lazy and crooked developers she had brought to financial destruction? Shit. All of it, shit. None of it mattered. She had done her best to ruin the life of the one person she truly loved more than any other human being. She knew why she was in that church: to continue to control Bonita Browne. But she had lost control, because she was a shit. A lying, self-deceiving shit. She was no different and no better than the drunks she had spent Christmas Day with in the county jail. She, and they, were shit.

Through her tears, Esperanza Lopez said, "No contest."

But Esperanza's humiliation had not reached completion. As she turned to walk out of the courtroom and to the bailiff's station for further instruction on where and how to sign up for counseling, she saw the face of Antonio. Her son had witnessed the trifecta: The third of the lowest three moments in her life. The mouth taping, the slapping of Bonita, and now the no contest plea. Only he knew, fully knew, about her total shittiness.

Esperanza turned her head away and stifled her sobbing. But when she got away from the courtroom and felt certain that Antonio was nowhere in sight, Esperanza began to sob uncontrollably.

Antonio didn't see the scene, however. He sobbed uncontrollably himself, in a different part of the courthouse.

XXII

Professor Dockett and Antonio worked together on the *United States v. Beau Ezekiel Browne* appeal. They discussed how to put the appeal together.

"Professor, shouldn't we put the First Amendment issue first?"

"Yes, but as I see it, you have three First Amendment issues. Number one, is the Fourth Circuit wrong? Shouldn't ministers, priests and rabbis just automatically be considered immune from prosecution when they take in any downtrodden human being? Number two; if the Fourth Circuit isn't wrong, should the Congregational proclamation in this case apply retroactively to January 23, 2051, per the church's intent? Shouldn't that distinguish this case from the Fourth Circuit case? And number three; was Hixson wrong to express his opinion in the jury instruction that the church cannot create a retroactive proclamation?

"Aren't numbers two and three the same argument?" asked Antonio.

"No. The distinction is that #2 is an argument as a matter of law. #3 is an argument that it's a matter of fact, and the jury should be permitted to decide whether the proclamation applies."

"But Professor, there was no evidence presented that the Congregational elders didn't intend to apply the proclamation retroactively. Shouldn't that mean that the question really is a matter of law, not a matter of fact?"

Professor Dockett paused. "Mr. Browne-Katich, that is an excellent point. Another 'A' for you. And between you and me, I agree with you. But the question is whether our Circuit Court of Appeals will agree with us. You see, here's the problem. We've just finished the briefing in the *Monroe* case. There, as I told you earlier, Bishop Monroe didn't testify, and there, no witness like a chief elder of the Methodist Church in Fort Worth testified to any proclamation. We've raised issue number one to the Fifth Circuit. We didn't raise numbers two and three, because in *Monroe* we didn't have the situation of a debate over the jury instruction as a result of testimony of someone like the chief elder, and we certainly didn't have the problem of the Texas judge commenting on the evidence. If the Fifth Circuit falls in line with the Fourth Circuit, we're done. Our Circuit will really not want to create a 'Circuit Split' in that instance. So, we have to keep that third issue in, so that we have a way to distinguish not only the Fourth Circuit but also the Fifth Circuit."

"I get it now, Professor! That's great! That's great thinking!"

"I thought so," said the pleased Dockett. "Now, issue #4 has to be the "enemy of the State" instruction. And thanks to your hard work, Antonio, we have a good record on that one."

"But Professor, if the Fifth Circuit rules against Bishop Monroe on that issue, won't our Circuit fall in line on the same logic?"

"Hmm. That's a good point, and your answer is 'probably.' But if the Fifth Circuit agrees with Bishop Monroe that a jury alone should decide who an 'enemy of the State' is, we look bad in raising the issue to Hixson, only to punt it to the Circuit Court of Appeals, when it's a winning issue. I think we raise it. And the beauty of that issue comes from the questions that the jury came up with during deliberation. That makes it tough for the government to argue that the error in not instructing the jury on 'enemy of the State' was harmless."

Antonio thought, *the jury? No, those questions came from my beautiful, intelligent wife. But only I know that. Let's not leave the impression with the Circuit that if the jury had been instructed on 'enemy of the State,' they would have returned a guilty verdict anyway. The reality is that those other 11 were like sheep. But the Circuit Court of Appeals won't know that!"*

"Okay, Professor, that's the next issue for sure. But what about a torture issue?"

"I don't see a legal issue there. You won that point, and you got the jury instruction you wanted on involuntary confessions. We didn't file a motion to suppress the confession. I'm not seeing how we raise that."

Antonio had thought it through, especially after having spoken with his wife numerous times about the matter: "We raise it this way: Even though we didn't file a motion to suppress, the Circuit should take it upon themselves to hold that whenever the police go to interrogate a suspect, intending to arrest him and book him into civilian court, and intending to torture him, it doesn't matter when the suspect talked relative to the torture; the whole statement should be suppressed. And if the confession is the only definitive evidence they have that Uncle Beau intended to harbor an enemy of the State, then the whole conviction should be thrown out."

Professor Dockett had also thought it through, however. "Here are the two problems I see with that. First, assuming for sake of argument you're right, the SCOTUS has long held that evidence is sufficient to sustain a conviction, even when it should have been suppressed and without the suppressed evidence the Government would not have had a case. The second problem I have with that is we would raise the issue as a matter of plain error, because we made the tactical decision not to file a motion to suppress."

"But it is plain error, Professor! Plainly, at least to me, when the police intend to torture someone, it shouldn't matter when the suspect confessed relative to when he was tortured!"

Dockett thought some more. "I see the Circuit getting around the issue by saying that it's the kind of plain error that they will not reach. I think that we have some strong issues in this appeal, and I hate to load the brief up with issues we can't win upon."

Antonio's eyes flashed. He and his wife had talked for hours about this issue. He knew how his wife felt. To her, this was the most important aspect of Beau Browne's case. Antonio felt he owed it to his wife, at the very least, not to give up on this issue.

"Professor, how about we compromise and make this the last issue? And I'll write it by myself. Remember, this issue also distinguishes our case from the *Monroe* case and also the Fourth Circuit case. Bishop Monroe and the other minister weren't tortured. If the Circuit wants to reverse the conviction but doesn't want to create a Circuit split with the Fourth and Fifth Circuits, this issue would give them another way to do so."

"You're on to something, Antonio. You're thinking like an appellate lawyer. I agree; we compromise. But as I see it, if that's our last issue, our second-to-last issue would be the misconduct your Judge Hixson engaged in, and why it warrants a new trial. I'm talking about how he caused your mother's mouth to be taped in front of the jury and then insulted her to the jury, and how he held me in contempt in front of the jury for things he said, and not I. I was thinking the same thing: If the Circuit wants to find a way to reverse the conviction and to distinguish the Fourth Circuit case, as well as the Fifth Circuit case if Bishop Monroe loses, this would be a way to do that! In fact, it really would be a better way, because there isn't any SCOTUS precedent against us on that issue!"

Antonio replied, "But professor. If Bishop Monroe loses, and we win only on this point, then we will have won a new trial where the law will be so against us that it will be impossible to win!"

Dockett had thought it through. "To the jury, that may be true. But if we win the appeal on the basis of judicial misconduct, that may give us a basis to file a motion to dismiss, after the Court of Appeals sends the case back to Hixson, on the grounds of double jeopardy. It's a hard motion to win. We have to prove judicial misconduct that was designed to prevent a defense verdict. But based on how unbalanced your Judge Hixson has acted, if we win a new trial I'll bet he'll engage in more goofy antics like he has done already! He'll do that in order to increase the odds of a second conviction. When he does, that will give us that double jeopardy motion later on down the road!"

Antonio looked at the Professor with admiration. He had never met anyone in his life quite as smart as Professor Fred Dockett.

And so, the two wrote the briefs: The three sub-issues on the First Amendment, the enemy of the State argument, the judicial misconduct/fair trial argument, and the "torture is never acceptable at any time" argument as the final argument.

Shortly after filing the last brief in the *Browne* case, Professor Dockett argued the *Monroe* case to the Fifth Circuit. Shortly after the argument Antonio called Dockett. "How did it go?"

"It was terrible. I have a gut feeling Bishop Monroe is going to lose. We drew the most law-and-order panel of three judges on the Fifth Circuit that we could have drawn. The only real hope for your Uncle Beau is that the Fifth Circuit doesn't decide the appeal until after your Circuit decides his. Not too likely, but it could happen. I just hope one circuit doesn't sit around and decide to wait until the other decides first, and they talk to each other before deciding!"

"Professor, are you saying that you think that both Uncle Beau's and Bishop Monroe's cases are ultimately going to go to the SCOTUS?"

Dockett sighed. "You can count on it!"

Antonio went home and tried to explain all of this to his Serbian wife.

"So," said Ana, "You are saying this, I think. The Fourth Circuit has declared the law is not corrupt, even though it is corrupt. Professor Dockett thinks the Fifth Circuit will agree with the Fourth Circuit. And if they do that, your Circuit will be too scared to disagree with them. For that reason your Circuit will also declare the law is not corrupt. That means that both your Uncle Beau and Bishop Monroe will die in prison for violating a corrupt law."

Antonio again was amazed at how perceptive and how clear his wife's thinking could be. "That's exactly what Professor Dockett and I are saying, unless the SCOTUS decides to hear the case and disagrees with all three Circuits. And that's not very likely at all. Remember, this is the same SCOTUS that thought the law wasn't unconstitutional, and it meant that you didn't have to know you were harboring someone who is an enemy of the State."

Ana shook her head. "We have to do something about this. This isn't right."

With dejection, Antonio responded. "But what? Deacon Joe Green has given all of these sermons nationwide about how corrupt the law is, and it doesn't seem to have made a difference. Facebook has run all of these memes about how wrong torture is and how wrong the DOJ's definition of 'enemy of the State' is, and it doesn't seem to have made a difference. All of these on-line newspapers and periodicals have spoken out against the Super Patriot Act of 2049, and it doesn't seem to have made a difference. People have paid their taxes in old wrapping paper wrapped in old fish and moldy bread, and it doesn't seem to have made a difference. We now are officially the most heavily incarcerated nation in the history of the world, and it doesn't seem to have made a difference. The prosecutor pointed out to you that local police forces have been using army tanks and military weapons to knock down the homes of suspected criminals for 50 years now, and nobody bats an eye at it. The jury certainly didn't. It didn't make a difference."

Ana Katich from Serbia jutted her jaw and her eyes flashed. "That's all true, Antonio. And it will never change unless we –- you and I -- do something about it."

"Like what?"

"Come up with something! I did not marry you because you are handsome, because you are rich, because you are charming! I married you because I know you can find a way to change this! I married you because you can make a difference to people in this world! Do you understand?"

Antonio gulped. His wife, Ana Katich, signed up for a husband who would throw himself into the legal machinery of social decay and make it stop, or die trying. This did not sound like the recipe for a long and happy marriage, with the end of days spent rocking on the front porch of a bungalow on the beach somewhere, with the warm glow of a summer sunset caressing their backs. But when the most beautiful woman in the entire world agrees to marry you, you do what she asks. You meet the challenge. You leap into the machine, hand in hand, together. And if you die, if the FBI and the NSA squish you like ants thirsting for water, they squish you together. You die, in love, together.

"Let me call Deacon Joe Green and talk to him. I have a way to reach him."

But Deacon Joe Green spoke personally with Antonio, and this time he had a much different tone in his voice:

At one point right after Pastor Browne's trial, Deacon Joe Green had prepared himself to spring into action. After his sermons on the Super Patriot Act of 2049, he had an ally in Sonny Stix, a wealthy Libertarian agribusiness man. Stix believed that the government's policies, up to and including the Super Patriot Act of 2049, had caused America's problems for decades. Deacon Joe Green had prepared to organize a march on Washington, funded by Sonny Stix, and to give a speech that was a variation on Dr. King's famous speech entitled, "I have a nightmare: The American nightmare." Further, he had prepared to advocate that all Americans pay only 85% of their taxes to the IRS, as a symbolic way of refusing to fund the moneys for the Corrections Corporation of America. Here's why he didn't do that:

It seemed that Deacon Joe Green's plea to pay taxes in wrapping paper wrapped with rotten fish and moldy bread hit a chord with a considerable number of Americans. Many Americans did just that. This royally annoyed the IRS. And Deacon Joseph D'Anthony Green discovered a major truth: If you act ostentatiously in America and annoy people, the one earthly enemy you do not ever want to make, much less annoy, is the IRS. If the FBI and the NSA can't get you, the IRS can and will. Consider Al Capone, just as one example. Or Joe Conforte as another.

In the case of Deacon Joe Green, the FBI and the NSA wiretapped his phones and hacked his computers, and discovered what he and Stix were planning. Unfortunately for the G-men, what Green and Stix were plotting was not illegal. So, they then enlisted the aid of the IRS. And the IRS discovered that a number of poor people who otherwise couldn't pay the admission into the Calvary Jamboree Park were paying "in kind," bartering with clothing, with books, with whatever property they could get their hands on. And the accountants hadn't properly placed value on the bartered goods, at least not in the opinion of the IRS, and in some cases failed to report the bartered goods at all. The IRS had turned this situation over to the Criminal Investigation Division of the IRS. The DOJ somewhat interceded, and struck a deal with Deacon Joe Green: They could indict him for tax fraud and send him to prison for certain under the US Sentencing Guidelines if he pushed it. But so long as he shut up about The Super Patriot Act of 2049 and any other form of civil disobedience, and just stuck to The Bible in his weekly sermons, they wouldn't indict him. With the statute of limitations not running out until April of 2058, Joe Green had to "behave himself" until then. And if he lost listener market share as a result of losing a little bit of his flamboyance, well, that's what you get for being a reprobate. That's life in America, you know?

Deacon Joseph D'Anthony Green had fought the law, and the law not only had won, it had crushed him like a fermented grape.

Antonio feared reporting this to Ana, and when she asked him about Deacon Joe Green, he stammered even more than he had at the buffet. Ultimately, Ana got the story out of Antonio. She took him by the hands and said,

"Antonio, I have two things to tell you.

You are afraid because you fear my reaction. You think I will think you are a weak man. You are not a weak man. I would not fall in love with a weak man. But I fell in love with you. You agreed to help your Uncle Beau. You looked for help when that judge and your mother put you in the position of not being able to help your Uncle Beau by yourself. You stood up to your mother when she beat your momma. Those are not the actions of a weak man. Those are the actions of a strong man.

The second thing I have to tell you is this: Now that I have thought about it some more, I understand that you have a job to do in being your Uncle Beau's lawyer. You have to work within the justice system. You have no power in what you do for a living if you work outside the justice system. I never should have asked you. I was wrong to do so.

I will do this the Serbian way. I will call on my older brothers, Goran and Petar. We will find a way to fight this injustice on our own."

XXIII

Antonio and Fred took the Musk Mobile to the Circuit Court of Appeals. There a throng of media, well-wishers, and celebrity-hunters met up with them. The nation watched, if not the whole world.

The most important day in the life of any federal appeal happens about seven days prior to the oral argument, when the lawyers discover the identity of the three judges on the panel deciding the case. In this case, Dockett, Browne-Katich and Atkinson drew the most interesting panel imaginable:

The first judge on the panel was Judge Silverberg. He was one of the few remaining old-style liberals left in the Circuit Courts of Appeal nationwide. President Hillary Clinton had put him on the bench in 2021. As the years wore on, Silverberg became more and more crotchety, and more and more critical of the US Government. Every time those ivory-towered nitwits on the SCOTUS reversed him just made him even more crotchety. Silverberg's name caused defense lawyers to cheer, prosecutors to shudder.

The second judge on the panel was Judge Brzezinski. President Jeb Bush, Jr had put Brzezinski, a libertarian, on the bench. But the judge that Bush thought he had stuck the Circuit with evolved into someone quite different. After attending and witnessing a botched execution, Brzezinski became transformed. She became more sensitive to the cause of civil liberties and individual rights as the years wore on. However, Brzezinski, a pragmatist, enjoyed her reputation as the canniest judge on the Circuit. Many judges would follow her lead whenever a controversy emerged.

The third judge was Judge Law. A far-right wing judicial conservative put on by President Rubio in 2035, he had proven himself as the most unpredictable judge on that Circuit. He also had proven himself as generally the Circuit's least collegial judge. Where possible, he would write dissenting or concurring opinions. Lawyers often spoke of the memorable time when Silverberg and Law clashed so sharply that Law began his dissenting opinion with "I respectfully disagree with everything my brother Silverberg has said, from the first word 'The' to the last word 'Reversed.' And I dissent from his use of every comma, every period, and every question mark in between."

Most likely, Dockett and Atkinson's jobs consisted of persuading Brzezinski.

Dockett approached the podium. Brzezinski, the presiding judge, nodded. Dockett spoke,

"If it please the Court, my name is Frederick Dockett and I represent Pastor Beau Ezekiel Browne. This case raises the vital question: Can an ordained minister take into his home someone who happens to be a convicted felon who never was, but theoretically could have been imprisoned, when that person needs habitation, and be immune from prosecution under the Super Patriot Act of 2049?"

Immediately, Brzezinski interrupted and cut to the heart of the case: "Counsel, are you advocating a Circuit split with the Fourth Circuit?"

"To tell the truth, your Honor, it is my personal belief and opinion that the Fourth Circuit is dead wrong, and interestingly, at least one of the jurors in this case evidently agrees, based upon the questions posed during deliberation. But you do not have to so rule in order to reverse."

Judge Law interrupted both of them: "Counsel, we understand your position. You are saying that this case is different from the Fourth Circuit opinion, because here we have the Elders of your client's church signing a proclamation, two days after your client was arrested, in essence justifying what your client did under their interpretation of the Holy Bible. But is it proper for the church to do that? Or is that just self-interested survival?"

Dockett replied: "From a religious perspective, we can debate the question all day long and never get anywhere. But from a legal perspective, how can we second-guess the wisdom of the governing body of a church?"

Law responded: "As to Congregational pastors who follow after Pastor Browne, I agree. But how can we allow that proclamation to apply retroactively?"

And Dockett rejoined: "Because if the governing body of the church tells all concerned that the proclamation clarifies what the tenets of that church have always meant, that is no different than this Court interpreting a statute to declare what the statute substantively has always meant. In either case, the interpretation takes effect the day the statute was passed, or in this case, the original charter created long before 2049."

Thoughtfully, Brzezinski responded: "What I find so interesting about this situation is that the jury was instructed on this very point, and yet Judge Hixson gave his opinion that the proclamation could not be applied retroactively. But then he told the jury that they weren't bound by his opinion. Was he wrong to do that?"

"Absolutely."

"Why?"

"Because he commented on the evidence."

Law responded, "Did he really? If he gave an opinion and then told the jury, 'You're not bound by my opinion,' is that really commenting on the evidence?"

"Absolutely."

"Why?"

"Because a judicial opinion by a trial judge is no different than a jury instruction, if you think about it. And in this case what Judge Hixson was telling the jury was, 'here's a jury instruction that defines the applicable law for you, but in my opinion you can ignore it.'"

Brzezinski mused, "You know, in all my years, I've never seen a trial judge do that."

Dockett laughed. "Your Honor, I have to say, I may be one of the few lawyers appearing before you who can legitimately say, 'I have more years behind me than you do,' and I've never seen a federal trial judge do that, either!"

That broke the tension somewhat. But then Law responded:

"But the Jury Instruction No. 13 may have been wrong for a different reason. Isn't the question of retroactivity of a proclamation a question of law rather than a question of fact? To use your analogy, a jury doesn't decide whether a statute applies retroactively. A judge does that. Why would it be different here?"

Dockett responded, "Well, your Honor, I agree with you to this extent: I can't imagine a trial where someone from a legislative counsel bureau would come before the jury and explain the meaning of the governing statute, independent of a jury instruction. But in this case, the Elder was allowed to testify over objection and the proclamation was introduced into evidence over objection. I submit for your consideration that for those reasons, retroactivity of the proclamation was in fact a question of fact for this jury to decide."

And Brzezinski responded: "As questions of fact go, there wasn't much of a question. The Government didn't present a witness to rebut the Elder, did it?"

"Certainly not."

"Then isn't it really a question of law?"

Dockett paused. Insofar as he was concerned, Brzezinski had just asked the key question. He was prepared to answer it: "It's a question of fact that really isn't in dispute. It's like a trafficking in methamphetamine trial, where there is no question that the intercepted substance is methamphetamine, and the defense is entrapment. The evidence of the existence of methamphetamine still has to be brought out in order for the Government, in that case, to meet its burden of proof."

Brzezinski got an "Aha!" look on her face. Law frowned, and said, "Unless there are further questions from the others, let's go on to your 'enemy of the State' argument. I understand your position. One of the elements of the Super Patriot Act offense is that your client harbored an enemy of the State. You say that the jury should have the final say on whether the person harbored is an enemy of the State. But doesn't that interfere with the executive branch's right to make that call?"

Dockett responded: "Not at all. Your Honor: From time immemorial, the whole point of a jury system, from the Magna Carta on forward, is to allow the common man to decide what the facts of a given case are, not the king."

And Law responded: "But the issue of 'enemy of the State' isn't a question of fact; it's a legal status. Isn't that right?"

Dockett had debated this one with Antonio in preparing for oral argument, and had this response: "If you think about it, it's an opinion. In the opinion of the federal government, Adam Kolkoski is 'an enemy of the State.' In the opinion of Pastor Browne, Kolkoski is not. In any trial involving competing opinions, such as the value of land that the government wants and has to pay for in a condemnation case, the jury decides which opinion carries the most weight. Why would that be different here?"

But Law had thought this one through as well: "Because this is about more than what an acre of land where a freeway would go might be worth to the landowner. This is about national security. How can we question the wisdom of the federal government on matters of national security?"

And Brzezinski said, "And how can we question the wisdom of a church that defines what its leader can do with a so-called 'enemy of the State'?"

Bingo. On that note it was tempting for Dockett to sit down and watch the show with Atkinson. But he had one more salvo to fire:

"And, on that theme, how can we question the wisdom of a judge who causes the taping of the mouth of an attorney in front of a jury, and holds another attorney in contempt in front of the jury for something the judge said? I submit that all of that is more than questionable; it is outrageous!"

Law responded. "I understand, Mr. Dockett, why your ego is bent out of shape on that point, and why your predecessor counsel's ego might have been bent out of shape as well. But wasn't all that just a harmless sideshow? Do you really think all of that affected the jury? Your jury was out for 13 hours of deliberation, and asked some really interesting questions, I must say. From the looks of it, your jury wasn't concerned about any of that."

And Dockett responded: "And in the end, when the judge wouldn't answer any of those really interesting questions, what did the jurors have to fall back on? They had to fall back on the specter of a trial judge disparaging not just one, but two defense lawyers, and in outrageous ways besides; and they had to fall back on a jury instruction that in effect told the jury that the defense really didn't have a defense, in the opinion of the judge. How can anyone call that a fair trial? When a judge displays this 'nudge, nudge, wink, wink' and 'slice, dice, not once but twice' type of attitude, as this judge displayed, doesn't that send a message to the jury to convict regardless of the evidence? I certainly think it does, and that among other reasons is why I say this judgment of conviction should be reversed. And to end on the note that Judge Brzezinski started, Judge Hixson's antics in this trial certainly distinguish this case from the Fourth Circuit case. The trial judge there certainly didn't 'deal the cards from the bottom of the deck' like this judge did."

Dockett sat down, curious about the fact that Silverberg hadn't said a word. This wasn't like him. But Dockett didn't have to wait much longer.

Dockett watched Atkinson as he got up to speak, "If it please the Court, my name is…"

"Counsel!" Thundered Silverberg, not allowing Chet Atkinson even to finish stating his name. "How can we tolerate a system of law in this country that allows the Government to torture a man of the cloth for following the commands of his religion, in this case the commands of Jesus Christ as set forth in the Gospels? This is the most outrageous thing I have ever seen in my 32 years on this bench!"

"Well, your Honor, the defense didn't file a motion to suppress, so…"

Silverberg wasn't through bellowing. "I know they didn't do that! But I don't care! My question to you is very simple: How can we tolerate a system of law in this country that allows the Government to torture a man of the cloth for following the commands of his religion, in this case the commands of Jesus Christ as set forth in the Gospels?"

"Well, the Roberts Court said…"

Silverberg was still not through bellowing, as he interrupted: "I know what the Roberts Court said! But this case was never considered to be a military case! Ever! This was an FBI investigation from the very beginning. And it is very clear to me that this so-called SISTER Act with the cute nicknames of 'Gloom', 'Doom', and 'Boom' if necessary, were going to torture this man of the cloth no matter what he said or what he did. I must ask you again, one more time: How can we tolerate a system of law that allows the Government to torture a man of the cloth for following the commands of his religion, in this case the commands of Jesus Christ as set forth in the gospels?"

Atkinson looked at Silverberg, and as evenly as he could say so, stated, "Your Honor, you have your answer to your own question. May I try to answer it for the benefit of Judges Law and Brzezinski?"

Silverberg responded: "You may try, but I have to say, counsel: I have never seen the Government in a worse position than this! It pains me to see our Government doing the things it did to Pastor Browne!"

Antonio tugged on Professor Dockett's sleeve, and whispered to him: "This isn't an oral argument; this is divine providence!"

Dockett smiled and put up his hand, as if to say, "I'm thinking here, don't interrupt my train of thought."

Dockett found himself almost feeling sorry for his opponent. Atkinson had just been rendered speechless, at a time when the ticking clock (of 15 minutes and not a second more of oral argument per side for both sides) commanded speech. Chet turned somewhat helplessly to the other two judges: "Do you have any questions of me?"

Brzezinski, undoubtedly sensing Atkinson's discomfort, responded: "I think you have excellently briefed the Government's position, and I don't have any particular legal questions. But I do have kind of an odd question for you: You were there during this trial. When your Judge Hixson ordered the one lawyer's mouth taped shut, and held the other lawyer in contempt for an answer to a question, which actually came from the judge, and not the lawyer, what was your reaction at the time? How did you feel?"

Dockett held his breath. *What is Brzezinski getting at? Is that a softball question, or a 110 mile-per-hour fastball?* Atkinson answered truthfully:

"Your Honor, the Government's position, here as in all cases, is that all defendants on trial must receive a fair trial. In my opinion, what Judge Hixson was doing in those regards was the opposite of a fair trial. I did what I could to help him cure the errors."

"And your legal position is that he cured them. Correct?"

"Of course."

Crap, thought Dockett. *Brzezinski is going to let Hixson get away with his misconduct.* But then Brzezinski followed up:

"But how could you and he succeed? You were the one who suggested that Judge Hixson put that 'opinion' language in that jury instruction, and Judge Hixson obliged you. And you didn't seek a mistrial on behalf of the government when Judge Hixson acted up in front of the jury, did you?"

Atkinson responded, "No, but neither did the defense. And they are the ones who have the burden to seek a mistrial, not the Government."

"Really?" Asked Judge Brzezinski. "You have just told me that you felt, as an officer of the court and as the representative of the US Government, that you had an obligation to ensure that Browne receive a fair trial. Wouldn't that obligation include trying to put a stop to what struck you as an unfair trial?"

Wow – a question that was as sharp as a brand new kitchen paring knife. Dockett and Browne-Katich sat on the edge of their chairs. How would their opponent answer that question?

He answered it this way: "I don't know of any precedent that obliges the Government to go that far. If your decision is going to turn on that point, I'd request an opportunity to brief the matter further."

Brzezinski replied, "Well, it may or it may not. I don't know yet. What I do know is that Mr. Dockett has one vote for a reversal, but he needs two. Mr. Atkinson, you may sit down, now. I want to hear from you, Mr. Dockett. Explain to me and to Judge Law why and how we should reverse without creating a Circuit split."

Fred knew exactly what Brzezinski was getting at. She wanted a way to reverse the judgment of conviction, such that if the Government was to seek certiorari from the SCOTUS and the SCOTUS was to grant certiorari, the SCOTUS in turn wouldn't spank the Circuit and that crazy liberal judge, Silverberg, yet again.

"Your Honor, here's what you do. You reverse on an accumulation of trial error. The judicial misconduct that Judge Hixson engaged in was absolutely intolerable. No defendant should ever have to put up with the specter of that. You don't need further briefing from the parties to figure that one out. And giving an opinion about the state of evidence in a jury instruction, in effect telling the jury to ignore evidence it had just heard is absolutely intolerable as well. The trial judge in the Fourth Circuit case didn't do any of that. If you reverse on those grounds, I can't see any reasonable jurist disagreeing with you to that extent, and I cannot see the SCOTUS taking certiorari on this case to review that issue."

But the cagey professor went on: "But for the benefit of the parties, in the event the case must go to retrial, you should also hold that the jury should be allowed to decide whether Pastor Browne is in fact an 'enemy of the State'; the jury should be allowed to decide whether Pastor Browne was privileged to harbor Mr. Kolkoski per the proclamation; and the jury should be specifically instructed that it may disregard anything that might otherwise be deemed an admission or confession by Pastor Browne if it finds that the FBI entered Pastor Browne's parsonage with the intent to torture him from the onset."

"Very well," responded Brzezinski. "Thank you, counsel, for your excellent presentations, both of you. This case shall stand submitted for decision or other order of the Court."

Antonio and Dockett left the courthouse. As they walked down the marble steps toward the busy, one-way street with Ubers whooshing about in front of the 200-year-old mausoleum-like structure, the media pounced upon them: "What did you think of the oral argument?"

Dockett replied: "The panel asked some great questions of the lawyers. And hopefully, the panel will conclude, as I would conclude, that we provided them with some great answers." Dockett smiled at them, and then ended his remarks.

After the press conference, Antonio asked Dockett, "Professor, what do you think will happen, really?"

Dockett replied, with his usual measure of droll: "I think what will happen 'really' is you and I are going to go get a bite to eat."

"No, I mean the decision, Professor. What do you think the panel is going to do?"

"It's pretty obvious. Silverberg wants to reverse; Law wants to affirm; and Brzezinski wants to craft an opinion that won't be shot down by the SCOTUS when the loser files a petition for writ of certiorari."

"So does that mean Uncle Beau is going to win, or Uncle Beau is going to lose?"

Before Dockett could answer that question, he felt a tap on his shoulder. Atkinson called his name. "Fred, can I have a word with you, alone?"

"Sure, Chet. What is it?" They walked a block, away from anyone who could hear them, and together they sat on a metal bench near the sidewalk.

"I'm done. I'm done with the Department of Justice. I'm done. After the way Silverberg humiliated me with his rant, I'm done. I couldn't answer his questions. He knew I couldn't answer his questions. They were unanswerable. I feel like the lone survivor in a war zone, who just saw bombs dropped and buildings destroyed all around him. I'm done."

"You're resigning?"

"I'm resigning."

"An old warrior like you?"

Atkinson chuckled ruefully. "Well, you know the old saying amongst old warriors, like you and me. We may resign, but we never quit."

Dockett laughed, and patted Atkinson on his shoulder. "Well, old friend, I wish you well. You understand, of course, that it wasn't personal between you and Silverberg. It was too bad that the Attorney General himself wasn't here to hear the crusty old judge's tirade. He's the one who needed to hear it, not you. And now you get to go back to Washington and deal with the fallout from the shrapnel, so to speak."

"Not for long. I resign. I'm going to go find a job with some state agency. I'm going to prosecute murderers and child rapists. That's easier than this."

And Fred responded to his new old friend: "It's your choice. And I understand how you feel. Silverberg made you feel the same way that Hixson made me feel. You know, out-of-control judicial egos will do that to you. But you know what? For what it's worth, in my opinion it would be too bad if you resigned. There are a lot of lawyers out there who can prosecute murderers and rapists. But not too many can negotiate their way through the legal and the emotional intricacies of something like the Super Patriot Act of 2049. I'm thinking that if there is anyone at the DOJ who could cause the powers that be to pull their heads out of the sand and get real about prosecuting under that law, it would be you."

Chet responded to his friend: "Thank you, Fred, but I have to say: There isn't anyone."

XXIV

Two months later, Professor Dockett received a telephone call from a journalist who covered the courts, employed by Gannett Media. "What is your reaction to the decisions today?"

"What decisions?"

"Haven't you checked your e-mail in-box yet?"

"No. What was the decision?"

"It was a 2-1 decision, and it is the oddest decision I've ever seen."

"Who won?"

"You did."

"Wait! You mean that Pastor Beau Browne got the judgment of conviction reversed?"

"That's what I'm telling you."

The Professor whooped. "Fantastic! But tell me: On what ground?"

The journalist replied, "I won't quote you on your 'Wahoo's!' and your 'Whoopee's!' because you may not feel like cheering after reading the opinion. " "Huh?" said a stunned Dockett.

The reporter responded: "That's what's so odd. There are three separate opinions. Silverberg agreed with you on everything. Law didn't agree with you on anything. Law held that all misconduct that Hixson engaged in was harmless, because Browne was so plainly guilty. Brzezinski held that Browne didn't receive a fair trial because of the judicial misconduct, and reversed on that ground. She said she didn't need to reach any of the other issues. But she hinted that if she had to decide the other issues, she might well agree with Silverberg."

"So," said Dockett, "The bottom line is Browne gets a new trial, but we don't know from this decision if the new jury will be instructed either on the First Amendment or on 'enemy of the State,' or for that matter, on the timing of torture and a defendant's admission or confession, and if so, what those instructions might look like."

"That's right."

Dockett shook his head. "Well, reversal of a judgment is always better than affirmance. But didn't you just say 'decisions?'"

"I did. The Fifth Circuit also decided the *Monroe* case today."

"What did they do there?"

"A two-to-one decision. They affirmed. The majority held that there is no 'enemy of the State' defense that can be presented, and they sided with the Fourth Circuit on the 'First Amendment' defense. The dissent held for Bishop Monroe on the 'enemy of the State' defense, but agreed with the Fourth Circuit on the 'First Amendment' defense."

Dockett chuckled, somewhat cynically. "Do you want a quote on the record or off?"

"Okay, let's go on the record."

"I am extremely delighted for Pastor Browne, and extremely disappointed for Bishop Monroe. But I'm sure that, under all of the circumstances, the Supreme Court of the United States will have to settle these disputes."

The journalist lowered his voice. "Okay, Professor, what do you have to say off the record?"

Fred rolled his eyes. "This country, and the judges who shape its legal and moral policies, is schizophrenic. These judges are nothing but a bunch of egotistical fucking whack jobs!"

"Oh come on, Professor, you can't mean that!"

Dockett shook his head. "No, I mean exactly that! I remember early in my career some wise old lawyer once telling me, 'Fred, there's one thing you have to remember about the appellate courts: They're not final because they're fair; they're fair because they're final.' The longer I go on in this business, the more I believe that's the God's honest truth!"

The media didn't ask for a quote, on the record or off, from Pastor Beau Browne. But even if they had, they wouldn't have received anything. The Bureau of Prisons assigned Beau to US Prison Leavenworth, but in the least restrictive portion of Leavenworth. There, the Bureau of Prisons granted him e-mail privileges. And right away he e-mailed his wife, his children, and his attorneys: No visitors. It was just too painful. He couldn't bear the sight of family at this horrible place in the state of Kansas. And no phone calls. Hearing voices would be just too sad for him. He would communicate by e-mail only. And the Bureau of Prisons monitors whom the inmates with e-mail privileges can or cannot communicate with, and they would not allow prisoner communication by e-mail with the media.

One day, however, Browne received a letter from the oddest, most intriguing source: Michelle Dailey, the jail matron from the old county jail days. Beau had received plenty of "fan mail" before, most of it from female well wishers who wanted to be his pen pal or to marry him. After all, with the status of "the country's most prominent martyr" came a certain degree of sex appeal.

Beau, married for many years, ignored the fan mail. But not in this case. Michelle wanted to know if there was any way she could help Beau with his re-trial. Beau sent the letter back to Michelle with a cryptic, computer-printed message: "Call Antonio Browne-Katich," with his phone number.

She did, and they met.

"Hi, Ms. Dailey. How can I help you?"

Michelle responded, "No, the question is: How can I help you?"

Michelle looked around Antonio's office, to make sure no uninvited ears could hear her. Then she spoke: " Here is the problem: Giovanni Ribaldi is a crook."

Antonio relied, "Of course he is. What do you want me to do about it? Do you want me to sue him?"

"It's not that easy, Mr. Browne-Katich."

"What do you mean?"

Michelle continued: "Do you remember when Ribaldi was acquitted?"

Antonio laughed. "Anybody who was alive in 2051 remembers that!"

Michelle did not laugh. "After that happened, I quit my job at the jail."

"Why?"

Michelle did not relish telling the truth, as it made her look stupid. "While Giovanni and your Uncle were in jail, Giovanni convinced me that once he got out, we would start a production company together. He came up with the name of "G & S Productions." We were going to do a remake of the old porn classic, "Ilsa: The She-Warden of the S.S."

"Wasn't that already done?"

Michelle snorted. "If you have ever seen that piece of trash, like I have recently, you would know why the answer is 'no'. But anyway, I cashed in my 401K accounts from my jail job and invested the proceeds into the 'G & S Company.'"

"Oh, boy," responded Antonio. "I think I know where this story is going."

"Right. Stupid old me agreed to play the role of Ilsa. Of course, I was going under the stage name of 'Stephanie Stiletto.' But every time we started filming, something would happen. This emergency would arise, or that glitch would happen, or some other actor would forget to show up, and filming stopped. And so there I stood, time after time, in my leather corset, with my whips and my boots and my swastika patches, and with nobody to whip into submission."

Antonio couldn't help but laugh. "Didn't you just feel ridiculous doing that?"

Michelle didn't want to admit what a total fool she had been: "Well of course. But Giovanni convinced me that he knew the porn business inside and out, and we were going to make millions doing this." Finally, she lowered her head and said, in a choked up voice, "Yes, I know, I'm an idiot. You don't have to tell me."

Antonio responded, "That's good. That's half the battle. So what happened next?"

Michelle had a tough time making it through the next part of the story: "So after awhile I got suspicious, and I started to investigate. I know it took me way too long to do that. But you see, Giovanni Ribaldi was my lover. I'm sure your uncle told you this, but when the two of them were cellies, I would sneak into Giovanni's cell at midnight, while your uncle was asleep, let Giovanni out, we would go to the conjugal visit room, and we'd have sex there."

"No, Uncle Beau never told me that!"

"Unlike Giovanni, your uncle had some class, then."

Antonio responded, "My guess, knowing my uncle, is that he and Giovanni made some kind of deal to keep all of that secret, for some reason."

Michelle continued: "Whatever the case, it took me awhile to figure it out. But after tracing though the bank records and finding the other bank accounts, I discovered that Giovanni funneled my investment money to his new, real, secret lover, Mistress Payne."

"Mistress Payne! Isn't she the one…"

Michelle interrupted Antonio. "Yes, yes, yes. Mistress Payne was an exotic BDSM dancer, and she was the one who showed up at Giovanni trial on Giovanni's arm." Michelle wrinkled her nose and said in a low voice, "That bitch hung all over him like an aged barnacle!"

Antonio laughed at the vision. "So, she stole your money?"

"Not exactly."

Antonio scratched his head. "This is starting to get interesting!"

Michelle continued: "Mistress 'no Payne no Gain' double-crossed Giovanni. Giovanni thought he was so smart. Little did he know that he hooked up with a bitch who had ties to the Ukrainian Mob."

"Uh, oh. They say you never want to cross a Ukranian, much less the Ukranian Mob!"

Michelle rolled her eyes: "Tell me about it! So, in time, the Mob owned G & S Productions. And of course, stupid old me was the last one to know. And here was what finally tipped me off to the scam: Finally, "Ilsa: She-Wolf of the S.S." got to the public, but the "instant classic" starred Mistress Payne, not me, as the actress, Stephanie Stiletto, playing "Ilsa." All that time, and I got played for a fool! But it didn't matter anyway; all of the earnings from that rotten movie ultimately made their way through to the Ukraine."

"Really?" asked an interested Antonio. "How did that happen?"

"Some lawyer for Giovanni set up this brilliant scheme, buying all these off-the-shelf corporations and hiding the owners, and the owners of the owners, and then the owners of the owners of the owners. I don't understand what he did. I'm not sure if Giovanni understood what the lawyer did. It was one huge shell game, that much I can tell you."

Antonio responded, "But I'd have to know, I'd have to understand to be able to get any money back for you!"

Michelle looked at the young lawyer. "Mr. Browne-Katich, you don't think I'm so stupid as to sue the Ukranian mob, do you?"

Antonio felt his cheek turn flush. "I assumed that's where you were going with this."

"Uh, no."

"Then why are we having this conversation?"

Michelle continued on: "Because of what happened next."

"Go on."

And Michelle continued. "Here's the problem. The FBI had not begun to close its book on Giovanni. They wanted revenge after his victory in 2051. And to top matters off, the FBI had messed up by forgetting to microchip him with a GPS tracking device and place him into the government's central data base, like they do to all people released from jail or prison."

"Wow! Ribaldi's luck never seems to run out, does it?"

"You may think not, but listen further. So, they investigated and pursued Giovanni. They were bound and determined to get him.

And then, Mistress Payne manipulated Giovanni and a Ukranian mobster into a love triangle, and then double-crossed Giovanni. Giovanni came to me, crying, begging for help. And stupid old me went with Giovanni to south Florida where the mobster temporarily was located, to confront Mistress Payne. Giovanni told me that his plan was to confront 'No Payne no Gain's' lover at gunpoint, and get my money back for me. He told me he then was going to get rid of Mistress Payne, and Giovanni and I then would shoot a sequel, the remade "Ilsa: Harem Keeper of the Oil Sheiks," starring me as the new Stephanie Stiletto as Ilsa."

Antonio looked at Michelle with amazement. "And you fell for this?"

Michelle hated admitting she was a fool, but soldiered on: "I went to Miami because I so wanted to believe him. Even after all of this time and all of this proof that he is a liar, I wanted to believe him. I know, I was stupid. 'How could a jail matron fall for a con?' you ask. 'Haven't you run into cons before?' you ask. All I can say is 'Sure: But none like Giovanni. The cons I know get caught and go to prison. I thought Giovanni was too smart to get caught, and therefore wasn't a con.' You don't have to tell me: Stinkin' thinkin', I know.

Anyway, so we were in Miami together, when suddenly the Ukrainian mobster appeared on the scene. Giovanni was carrying a semi-automatic. He and the mobster had a shootout. I ducked by a wall and saw the whole thing. The mobster accidentally killed himself with a freak ricocheting gunshot."

"Okay, so you're in the clear, right?"

Michelle frowned. "Not exactly. You see, the mob thought that Giovanni and Michelle had killed him. You know, the mob doesn't exactly employ crime scene analysts on the spot to figure out what happened. They believe what they believe. And before you know it, both the Ukrainian mob and the FBI were after all three of us – Ribaldi, Mistress Payne, and me."

"Oh, boy," responded Antonio. "You have to cooperate with the FBI, starting now. I know how these things go. It's called 'the race to the courthouse.' The first one to the courthouse – meaning to the FBI – wins."

"Yeah, well, guess what, the race is over," responded Michelle.

"Oh, no!"

"Oh, yes! The FBI has already arrested Mistress Payne on murder, racketeering and money laundering charges. She won the race. She immediately turned government's evidence. Her story was that it was a plot to kill her Ukrainian lover, and Giovanni and I were in it from the get-go."

Antonio exclaimed with alarm: "That's a lie! Based on what you just told me, that's a lie!"

"Sure, but here's the problem: The FBI thinks it's the truth. They've made up their minds already."

"How do you know that?" asked the inquisitive Antonio.

"Here's how. The FBI got to me. I should have lawyered up, but stupid me, I talked. I told them 'No Payne No Gain' was lying out her ass. When they told me I was wrong, I suggested to the Agent that he must have been fucking her. Boy, was that ever the wrong thing to say! That agent told me in no uncertain terms that my life was over. He said my option was this: I could work with the FBI and go undercover, lure and bring Ribaldi in so he could be arrested."

"Would you do that?"

Michelle responded. "Giovanni isn't the problem any more. The Ukrainian mob is the problem. If I do that, I risk getting killed by the Ukrainian mob."

"So you're not going to do that."

Michelle said intensely: "It's not that easy. The FBI laid out my options. I bring them Giovanni, and I get a plea bargain that would have me serving only ten years; or I can tell them to leave me alone, in which case I will be indicted, arrested, and prosecuted to the max, and I will get a true life sentence."

"You're not going to get a true life sentence! You're innocent!"

Michelle practically shouted in disgust: "Jeez, Mr. Browne-Katich, how can you believe that after what you've been through with your uncle? The Government has its bullshit conspiracy theory to tie me into the murder of the mobster, and Mistress Payne's perjury that the jury naturally will buy off on, like the super-judgmental juries in our town always do after I'm tried and fried in the media before the trial, like they always do! Got it? The Agent told me, and he said it in a way that you can hear him now and believe him later: The Government will put me away for the rest of my life unless I start cooperating!"

"So, are you going to cooperate?"

Michelle paused, while she pondered. "I don't know. I've told them I will. But I'm trying to string them along. I don't know how much more time I have."

Antonio then queried, "This sounds like a great movie plot and all, but what does it have to do with me or with my Uncle Beau?"

Michelle replied: "When I was at the County Jail, I loved your Uncle Beau. He was so kind to me, and after all this time I still have feelings for Giovanni. Your Uncle Beau helped Giovanni to stay as sane in the jail as Giovanni could. And I felt so badly about how your Uncle Beau was railroaded by the FBI. I hate the FBI. They've ruined my life, and they've ruined his. If there's anything I can do to bring those bastards down and help your Uncle Beau, I'll do it."

Antonio thought about it. "I really can't think of anything you could do that would be pertinent to Uncle Beau's case. But talk to my wife, Ana Katich. Here's her number. She has something in mind; maybe she can figure out a way you can help."

XXV

After the Circuit Court of Appeals announced its decision, the Attorney General's Office announced theirs. They decided not to seek a rehearing before that Circuit full of right-brained, left wing goofballs; they determined to head straight to the SCOTUS.

Meanwhile, Bishop Monroe sought rehearing before the entire Fifth Circuit and ultimately the Fifth Circuit denied his motion. On behalf of Bishop Monroe, Fred Dockett announced that he, too, would file a Petition for Writ of Certiorari to the SCOTUS.

Under the Supreme Court rules, when the Circuit Court of Appeals (or the State Supreme Court, in the case of a petition from state court) issues its final order, telling all concerned that the appellate court is done with the case, the losing party has 90 days to file a petition for writ of certiorari. In this case, that made the Government's petition in *United States v. Browne* due a few months before the defendant's in *Monroe v. United States.*

On the 89th day of the 90-day period, the Solicitor General signed off on the petition and each of the 50 copies, and sent them to the mailroom of the Attorney General for service. The mailroom clerk sent the Petition out – to the US Congress. By the time a mailroom clerk at the Capitol Building figured out what was inside the big box and why, and redirected the box to the Clerk's Office of the SCOTUS for filing, it was the 95th day.

The Government's Petition for Writ of Certiorari could not be heard, absent a special order from the SCOTUS allowing it to be filed out of time.

By the time the Solicitor General investigated to discover the reason for the untimely filing, the mailroom clerk had quit and moved to San Francisco without comment, and moved underground in the Tenderloin District under an assumed name, where he could not easily be found. Did he misdirect the Writ Petition accidentally or on purpose? The issue reminded a few historians of Rosemary Woods' erasure of 18 minutes of the Watergate Tapes during the Watergate scandal in 1974. Did she do it accidentally or on purpose? Then, as now, forensic science hadn't been perfected to where the question could be answered to a reasonable degree of scientific probability based on the tape or the box alone.

Whichever the case, the SCOTUS denied the Government's motion to file the writ petition untimely. Without an affidavit from the mailroom clerk, the Government could not meet its burden on that motion. The Circuit Court of Appeals' decision in *United States v. Browne* was now final.

But Pastor Beau Browne remained at USP Leavenworth by agreement, pending the outcome of *Monroe v. United States*. Dockett and Browne-Katich agreed with the Government on one thing: Since Browne faced retrial and bail still wasn't legally possible, he was better off awaiting the result of the *Monroe* opinion in the awful USP Leavenworth than he would be in the even more awful county jail.

Six months later, Professor Dockett appeared in Washington and argued the *Monroe* case to the SCOTUS. The questions from the nine Justices came from all over the map. The argument seemed like a repeat of Silverberg, Law and Brzezinski, only threefold in number and intensity -- and this time, with no judicial misconduct, institutionalized torture or "opinionated" jury instructions as a backup. The issues before the SCOTUS were very direct: 1) Under the First Amendment to the US Constitution freedom of religion clause, is a minister, priest or rabbi automatically privileged to house someone defined as an "enemy of the State" by the Department of Justice, when that person is sick, injured, homeless, or reasonably appears to be persecuted by any state or federal government? 2) Under the Sixth Amendment to the US Constitution right to jury trial clause, does a jury have the ultimate authority to decide who an enemy of the State is in a prosecution brought per the Super Patriot Act of 2049? That is, can a jury override the Department of Justice's definition contained in the Code of Federal Regulations?

Four months later, the SCOTUS issued its opinion. The nation became swept into the controversy of the decision of *Monroe v. United States*.

Four of the Justices answered the questions "Yes" and "Yes." Three of the Justices answered the questions "No" and "No." The eighth and ninth Justices specially concurred with the "No" and "No" votes -- i.e., with the Government. In their opinion, they held that the questions litigated were not properly before the Court, because they were not raised precisely in that format to the Fifth Circuit Court of Appeals. Therefore, they would have dismissed the writ petition as improvidently granted, meaning the Court should not have granted certiorari in the first place. They expressed no opinion on the merits of the two questions before the Court.

The rule of law is that the holding of a case consists of any point of law that the majority of Justices can agree upon. In the case of *Monroe v. United States*, five Justices could not agree upon anything. The greatest number of votes sided with Bishop Monroe; but that was merely four in number. In terms of setting precedent, the opinion was useless.

Put another way: At the end of the proceedings, the bottom line was that Pastor Beau Browne was going to get another chance to clear his name; but nobody really knew what the governing law would look like precisely. But in the hands of Senior Judge Jonah Hixson, who hadn't clearly been proven wrong, it didn't look very promising at all for Pastor Browne. But at least Pastor Browne would get another chance.

But on the other hand, Bishop Monroe would die in prison someday.

And that, ladies and gentlemen, is what we call "justice."

When the decision came out, Fred Dockett called Antonio Browne-Katich. "Antonio: Do you remember that day on the sidewalk when Chet Atkinson told me he had had it, he was through?"

"Like it was yesterday, Professor."

"Well, that makes two old warriors ready for the park bench. I can't take it any more. I just don't have any fight left in me. The Supreme Court of the United States has succeeded in surgically removing 'the fight' from me. Teaching trial practice full time, to a bunch of eager young students who, some day, like Chet and Fred, will say 'I'm done; I can't take it any more,' sounds like what the doctor ordered for me. You are a young warrior. You're not anywhere close to the park bench yet, and you can handle this case on your own. You don't need me any more. You know this case, and you know how to try a case. You're 34-years-old. You're not an apprentice any more. It's time for you to spread your wings and fly. Just don't eat any fermented pyracantha berries on the way and fly into any windows!"

XXVI

If you ever want to see a trial judge in an angry state of mind, all you have to do is see him after one of his cases has been reversed by the appellate court, when he believes the jury reached the right decision. That means the appellate court has treated him to the specter of having to preside over the same damned jury trial again, where the new jury of course will find the defendant "guilty," like they always do. And when the appellate court bases the reversal on judicial misconduct that is a special form of sea salt rubbed into the wound. I.e., judges have egos, at least as big as lawyers'. Judges don't like to be spanked, any more or less than lawyers do.

In that state of mind, as soon as the SCOTUS announced its decision in the *Monroe* case, Jonah Hixson announced that the case of *United States v. Beau Ezekiel Browne* was set for retrial within two months. No continuances would be allowed for any reason except for deaths in the family -- and in that instance, the Honorable Hixson would need at least two weeks notice.

That didn't give Ana Katich very much time to do anything. But after Ana met with Michelle Dailey, Goran Katich and Petar Katich, she and they didn't need much time.

As the four talked about it, they realized how best to address the injustice that was the Super Patriot Act of 2049 and the FBI's enforcement of the same:

Michelle, as the former matron of the jail who regularly took both prisoners and jurors to and from the Federal courthouse, had an in with her old partner from the jail. Michelle made up a story about realizing she had left behind an old piece of jewelry somewhere near the back stairwell of the courthouse. The partner returned an old favor and told Michelle the new security entry code into the back part of the building, where the jurors arrived and departed on each judicial day. Michelle also knew what the security cards for entry into the building looked like, and still happened to have one in her possession. On the first day of the retrial, she popped open the back door at five in the morning for the Katich's. She also knew where the security cameras were, and explained the layout to Goran and Petar Katich.

Goran and Petar, dressed in all black, wore phony juror badges that Ana had also saved from her trial and designed on her computer, and the brothers had scarves, hats, and fake glasses hiding their faces while wearing rubber gloves. Goran immediately threw a black blanket over the nearest camera, so that it could not capture Michelle and Petar, scurrying up the stairs to the security room right behind Goran.

There, Michelle punched in the security code again, the door to the security room opened, and Petar, the systems analyst expert of the bunch, immediately figured out how to dismantle the security system so that it could not operate. Petar then sprinkled a vial of blood he had stolen from a medical laboratory on the console, so as to create a false forensic clue. He called it "The Blood of Tesla."

Upon Michelle's cell phone signal to Ana, Ana then came from outside and up the back stairs with about 150 fliers in a box. Michelle opened the jury deliberation room and the juror's entry into Judge Hixson's courtroom. Ana, Michelle and Petar distributed the fliers inside of the jury room, on every juror's seat, and upon every seat in the public section of the courtroom, where the prospective jurors would sit. Goran remained outside the courthouse door for security purposes, running counter-surveillance. In fact, when a federal security guard came around the corner, Goran tasered him with his stun gun. The guard remained motionless on the federal courthouse parking lot for several hours, until government employees discovered him there at the beginning of the workday.

To the back of each flier, the co-conspirators had placed a super-adhesive strip to the back, so that each flier could be affixed to each seat and not be removed without damaging each seat.

And each flier read as follows:

"Attention Jurors and Would-Be Jurors: You are about to be asked to apply an unjust, immoral law, the so-called Super Patriot Act of 2049, and convict a kind and gentle man, who did nothing but show kindness to someone who needed kindness. You should know your rights, because Judge Jonah Hixson will not explain them to you. You have the right to deliver a verdict that satisfies your conscience. And you have the right not to be punished for refusing to follow an unjust law.

The ability of a jury not to convict on an unjust law goes all the way back to the Magna Carta. Juries have applied their right to follow their consciences in trials throughout history to people such as William Penn and Wild Bill Hickok. This is called the right of jury nullification. Do you ever drink? You should know that, but for jury nullification, the Eighteenth Amendment never would have been repealed.

You should further be aware that you are being asked to return a verdict of guilty, when a majority of the Supreme Court of the United States could not agree on whether that was a proper result in a related case. If the Supreme Court of the United States cannot agree, then you should not consider yourselves to be bound to the law, as it will be given to you in jury instructions.

You should further know that the consequence of a guilty verdict would be life imprisonment. The sentence will be life imprisonment for one committing a kind act that harmed nobody, and was committed with no intent to harm the US Government. The judge cannot compromise; on a guilty verdict he can only impose a sentence of life imprisonment. Therefore, you should know that your guilty verdict would condemn a kind, Christian man who did nothing but a kind, Christian act to spend the rest of his life in prison. There is no parole in the federal system. And you will have to live with yourself and that verdict. It will bear down on your conscience every time you do an act of kindness. Know that it bore down on the conscience of the jury before you who followed this unjust law and found the Defendant guilty, before the Circuit Court of Appeals reversed that verdict.

You will not be told of your right to nullify an unjust law, such as the Super Patriot Act of 2049. But you have that right. You have that freedom. Exercise your right with wisdom, with kindness, and with compassion for your fellow human."

To put it mildly, when Hixson came to work and was alerted to the fliers, as well as the fact that every one of the prospective jurors had seen them, he went berserk. He immediately called for a hearing, with the jury panel waiting outside.

"You!" Hixson screamed at Browne-Katich. "You are behind this, aren't you? Your desire to win this case has overcome your common sense, hasn't it?"

Antonio reacted in a stunned state of mind, and he gulped: "I'm sorry, your Honor. I really don't know what you are talking about."

"Don't give me that!" snarled Hixson. "This flier says that the verdict weighed on the conscience of the last jury. I happen to know that the last jury had a juror that you later married. You prepared this flier, didn't you?"

Antonio's fear started to give way to indignation: "No, your Honor! I did not!"

"Then you aided and abetted your wife, who prepared this flier. You were the one who told her about William Penn, Wild Bill Hickok, and the Eighteenth Amendment, weren't you?"

"Your Honor, nobody tells Ana Katich what to do on anything, or how to do it. She's very smart. She knows how to read. She has a computer with Super Google."

Hixson bore in. "Aha! So, now you're telling me that Ana Katich, your wife, prepared this flier, correct?"

Antonio realized that Hixson was doing his best to get evidence out of Antonio. And maybe if Antonio hadn't grown up under the roof of Esperanza Lopez, he wouldn't have learned the fortitude to shut up before speaking, think, and then say what he said next. But one thing was for sure: Antonio Browne-Katich would go to prison for as long as he had to before he would subject his wife to harm. With determination and indignation, Antonio Browne-Katich looked at Judge Jonah Hixson and said this:

"Your Honor: If you are looking to have somebody prosecuted for obstruction of justice, I could and perhaps should take the Fifth Amendment. But I won't at this time, because I have nothing to hide. If you are looking to have my wife prosecuted for obstruction of justice, and to have me bear witness against my wife, I could and perhaps should exercise my privilege not to testify against her, and further exercise my right to claim my privilege against revealing spousal communications. But again, I won't because I have nothing relevant to say. I didn't see my wife create the flier, nor did she tell me that she was going to create the flier, was creating the flier, or had created the flier -- if in fact she created the flier.

And if you are looking to have anybody prosecuted for obstruction of justice for the act of creating and distributing this flier, regardless of who created and distributed this flier, let me just say two things. First, it would appear that whoever wrote this wrote statements of fact. From what I know of the principles of jury nullification, everything stated here is true. I don't see how the author of this flier could be prosecuted, consistent with the First Amendment right of freedom of speech. This flier could not reasonably be interpreted as a clear and present danger call to violence, or as anything fraudulent or even misleading.

Secondly, if what you are doing is looking to prosecute whoever wrote this, I would suggest to you that you have stepped out of the role of the presiding judge and taken a role consistent with the Department of Justice. And that tells me you are impliedly biased as a matter of law, and you need to recuse yourself from all further proceedings in this case!"

Hixson paused. One could practically hear the man fuming. In a low growl, similar to that of a rabid dog before a dog bite attack, Hixson said, "I am going to take a recess right now. I will decide what to do. Then I will reconvene court and give you my decision. I order you, young man, not to move from this courtroom. If you move anywhere from this courtroom, I will authorize the US Marshal to take you into custody, right then and there. I hope for your sake that you do not have to urinate!"

Hixson left the bench, slamming the door behind him. The first thing he did was head for the chambers door of Judge Norcross, his trusted colleague.

He explained the situation to Judge Norcross. "Edwin, what should I do?"

Judge Norcross paused and looked intensely at Hixson. "Jonah, do you want my honest opinion?"

"Yes. Let's hear it."

"Resign."

"What?"

"Resign. Recuse yourself."

"And let that young punk lawyer have his way? Never!"

"Listen to me, Jonah. You wanted my counsel, now you will hear it:

I read the Circuit Court of Appeals' opinion. Not only did they reverse you based on judicial misconduct, but also you engaged in the misconduct well after the Government began its case. And, it is clear to me with that jury instruction giving your 'opinion' on the law, that you did it with the intent of having the jury return a guilty verdict. I'm amazed that Dockett missed the issue. Your misconduct caused the jury to return the guilty verdict they returned. Dockett should have sought a dismissal after the return of the guilty verdict under the federal double jeopardy clause pursuant to *Oregon v. Kennedy*."

"What do you mean by that?" asked Judge Hixson.

"I'm talking about the theory of a violation of double jeopardy where, after the jury trial starts and jeopardy has attached, the prosecutor or the judge engages in misconduct, in order to ensure either that the prosecutor wins or the defense doesn't, and either a hung jury results or the judgment of conviction gets reversed on appeal on that basis" responded Judge Norcross.

"Well, but Dockett didn't file a motion like that," said Judge Hixson.

"Well, but Antonio Browne-Katich strikes me as an amazingly smart young lawyer. If you engage in one more act of judicial misconduct, you will hand him a motion to dismiss based on double jeopardy. As it stands, I think he might already have it from the first trial. Either way, he will file it. And to be brutally honest with you, based on what I heard you say out there just now over the loudspeaker, I think you are pretty darned close to engaging in one more act of judicial misconduct right now. If you do that, any judge – including me – would grant a motion to dismiss!"

"Edwin, do you really think I can't be fair?"

Judge Norcross looked at his old judicial colleague, and as evenly yet firmly as he could, said these words:

"I think it's time for you to resign."

Judge Hixson looked down. His lip started to quiver. He bit his lip, and turned his head away from Judge Norcross. Compassionately, Judge Norcross added:

"I have an idea, Jonah. I don't think there is a judge in this District that can hear this case. I know I already said I couldn't. I'm sure the rest of the judges in this District would be delighted to recuse themselves as well. In fact, the rest of them said to me that if they had been I, they would have done what I did after hearing Deacon Joe Green's sermon years ago. I will get with the Chief Judge of the District, and I will have him call the Chief Judge of the Circuit Court of Appeals. I will have the Chief Judge suggest to the Circuit Chief Judge that he assign Senior Judge Mendez from the District of Arizona to hear this case."

Judge Hixson looked up at Judge Norcross. "Mendez?"

"Yes, Mendez."

"What a wonderful thought! Mendez will see this case exactly as I do! Browne will have his 'fair trial' before a different jury, after I declare a mistrial, and that jury will convict Browne! Mendez will give him a life sentence! And I will be off the hook! That is positively brilliant, Edwin! Thank you!"

Judge Hixson re-took the bench, and brusquely stated his ruling:

"Based on the fliers and the jury panel's discovery of the contents of the fliers, I declare a mistrial and dismiss this entire jury panel. I also recuse myself on the basis of implied bias. I order that a transcript of this morning's proceedings be created as soon as possible. I order the transcript, as well as many of the fliers as can be collected, be transmitted forthwith to the FBI for further investigation. I further order that the US Marshal and the Court Services Officers get together and revise the security system in this building, so that there be no further successful break-ins. And I order the Chief Judge to reassign this case to a different judge."

The Chief Judge of the District indeed telephoned the Chief Judge of the Circuit. But Judges Norcross and Hixson had overlooked the identity of the Chief Judge of the Circuit: Judge Brzezinski.

Upon hearing the request for Judge Mendez, Judge Brzezinski said, "I will assign a new presiding judge. Understand that I am not bound to appoint Judge Mendez, but I will give his selection every serious consideration that it deserves."

About the time Judge Brzezinski hung up the phone she ceased giving Judge Mendez any consideration, serious or otherwise. She knew what that District was up to. Judge Brzezinski also knew how she would have really decided the *Browne* case, had she not had to worry about how the SCOTUS could spank her court yet again, and the Congressional fallout from yet another spanking – especially on the *Browne* case.

Rather than appoint Mendez, Brzezinski appointed Senior Judge Hiroshi Nakamura of Seattle, one of the most liberal and even-minded jurists in the USA.

At long last, Beau Ezekiel Browne was going to receive a fair trial.

XXVII

Several months later, the retrial really started. This retrial had no spectacle of educational fliers, although the media coverage regarding them put the fact of the fliers and their message in the community's collective consciousness for quite some time. Nakamura immediately distinguished himself as a kind, wise judge, who made his position very clear.

Prior to jury selection, Nakamura took the bench and told the lawyers: Pastor Browne would be given full permission to explore every defense he had. That meant the jury would be instructed on the First Amendment defense, without any "judicial opinions." The jury would also be instructed that it had the right to determine whom 'an enemy of the State' really is, and could consider but would not be bound by the Code of Federal Regulations. And the jury would be permitted to disregard everything Beau Browne said to the FBI, if the jury were to find that the FBI intended to torture Browne from the time the tank knocked down the front door of the parsonage.

"But your Honor," protested the new prosecutor, "That is patently unfair to the Government! The Government is entitled to a fair trial, too!"

Nakamura smiled at the prosecutor. "I don't know what the jury is going to do when it hears all the evidence and considers all of the legal theories on interpreting the evidence. But I know this much: This case is not going to be tried a third time! As for the charge that I am not being fair to the Government, my response is very simple: Do your best!"

Antonio Browne-Katich certainly did. Agent Gluck, who since had been terminated from the FBI over a different incident and now worked as the chief of security at some hotel-casino in Las Vegas, took the stand. He had laryngitis that day, and hadn't had a good night's sleep in a few days after a bikers' convention and the racket from 10,000 Harleys. Gluck's mood bore similarity to a German shepherd that had been chained up too tightly for too long. The cross-examination of Gluck went like this:

Q: Former Special Agent Gluck: When you and Agent Dombrowski approached my client's home, you intended to torture him, didn't you?

A: (snarling) No!

Q: Really? No? You leaped out of a tank, carrying an M-16A10 and wearing paramilitary gear, but you intended to play a little bit of Mah Jongg with the Pastor?

A: I intended to get to the truth.

The crowd murmured.

Q: And you had already determined 'the truth' in your mind before you said one word to him, isn't that right?

A: What do you mean?

Q: I mean, you had made up your mind before Pastor Browne said one word that he was harboring an enemy of the State, based on what you knew. Correct?

A: I knew he was harboring an enemy of the State, yes.

Q: So, you didn't need to talk with him, at all, correct?

A: No, I wanted to give him a chance to explain his side of the story.

Q: Oh, *Former* Special Agent Gluck, come on. You can tell the truth here. We're among friends here. You know? You had made up your mind to arrest Pastor Browne before you drove the army tank through the front door of his parsonage. Correct?"

The pause was dramatic. Everyone leaned in to see how Gluck would answer. Finally:

"Okay, yeah."

After an even louder crowd murmur, Antonio continued:

Q: So, tell me, then, what could Pastor Browne have said to you that would have made you change your mind?

A: I don't know.

Q: You don't know? You wanted to give him a chance to tell his side of the story, but you have no idea what side of the story he could have given you that would have made a difference?

A: That's right.

Q: All right. So, if you were going to arrest Pastor Browne, no matter what he had to say, why did you torture him?

A: Because the Roberts Court said it was permissible, counselor. You know that.

Q: Really? Let me show you the Roberts Court's opinion in question. Have you ever read it?

A: No.

Q: What?? You think the opinion of the United States Supreme Court gives you the right to engage in what some consider to be a human rights violation, and you've never even read the opinion??

At this point the crowd murmur was even louder.

A: I already answered that question, counselor!

Q: May I approach the witness, your Honor?

Nakamura: Certainly.

Q: Read the opinion right now, Former Special Agent Gluck. Take all the time you need. We have time. Just read the headnotes, if that's easier for you. All right? Tell me where in this decision Chief Justice Roberts said that it is all right for the FBI to torture an American citizen, much less a minister, priest or rabbi, who has no intention to overthrow the United States Government. Can you point me to where Chief Justice Roberts ever said that?

Gluck started to growl. The crowd gasped in anticipation of his answer:

A: No.

Q: In fact, he never said that. Isn't that true?

Gluck growled more loudly.

A: Yes.

Browne-Katich, energized by the public in the courtroom, was practically in Gluck's face.

Q: Former Special Agent Gluck: Isn't it a fact that you thought the FBI had given you permission to torture Pastor Browne?

A: Yes.

Q: And isn't it a fact that the reason you tortured him is because you *enjoy* torturing folks?

Gluck didn't answer. He was about ready to explode, as was the public. The prosecutor objected. Nakamura overruled the objection and directed Gluck to answer. He still wouldn't answer.

Q: Former Special Agent Gluck. Evidently you didn't understand my question. It's not that hard to understand: Did you torture my client because you *enjoy* the act of torture?

The public tittered loudly. The prosecutor objected. Nakamura overruled him, and again directed Gluck to answer the question.

In a very measured voice, Gluck said, "I tortured your client because he harbored an enemy of the State!"

Q: And you *enjoy* torturing people who harbor people whom you believe are enemies of the State, don't you?

And...Kaboom! Gluck exploded. "Listen, you little punk! That's a stupid question! You have no idea of the kinds of things I did for you little wise-asses while I worked at the FBI to give you and your little punk-ass friends your freedoms! Don't you get all squishy liberal with me! I'm sick of you whiny liberals who think you know everything!"

Antonio turned to Nakamura: "Your Honor, would you direct the witness to answer my question?"

Nakamura chuckled. "I would, but apparently he doesn't want to, no matter what I might tell him to do!"

Antonio replied, "Then, I will ask another one. Former Special Agent Gluck: Suppose you think that someone is harboring an enemy of the State, but it turns out you're wrong. Do you still enjoy torturing that person?"

Gluck answered in his raspy voice:

"I'm never wrong."

Nobody could miss the loudness of the public's gasp. Antonio had notes on other questions to ask Gluck, but he put his notes down. If this didn't convince the jury to acquit his Uncle Beau, nothing else would. He had just proven that the FBI terminated the employment of Former Special Agent Gluck for one basic reason: The man was a monster. Anybody and everybody, prosecution- and defense-minded alike, could see it. The media's talking heads were going crazy with their daily report that day of the trial.

At the first break, Ana Katich, who was seated in the front row, came up to Antonio and hugged him. "Oh, Antonio, this is what I wanted you to do! I knew you could do it! I'm so proud of you!"

Antonio Browne-Katich: America's lawyer. He was on the brink of winning the biggest case in the country.

Even so, Antonio believed he could not win it unless Beau Browne took the stand and testified. He believed, even with the rest of the evidence, including the Congregational Elders' proclamation, and the favorable jury instructions to follow, that the jurors needed to see for themselves the kindness and gentle manner of his Uncle Beau. They needed to feel the impossibility that Pastor Beau Browne would ever do anything to harm the United States of America.

Triumphantly, Antonio Browne-Katich announced, "The defense calls Pastor Beau Browne."

Beau froze. He waved his hand, as if to say, "no." Stunned, Antonio waved his hand toward the witness stand, as if to say, "What do you mean, 'no'? Get up there!"

Beau walked very slowly and unsteadily to the witness stand, almost falling, and turned toward the jury.

"Please state your name for the record, and spell your last name."

Silence.

Antonio repeated, "Please state your name for the record, and spell your last name."

Silence.

Judge Nakamura interrupted, "Pastor Browne, are you able to state your name for the record?"

Beau shook his head in the negative.

Judge Nakamura turned to Antonio. "Let's take a brief recess. Counsel, talk to your client and find out what's going on."

As the jury and the judge left the courtroom, Antonio approached the Pastor and said, "Uncle Beau, what the devil is going on?"

Beau pointed to the legal pad and pen on the counsel table. Antonio gave them to Beau, and he wrote. The handwriting was so sloppy that Antonio could barely read it.

"Stroke?"

Beau nodded.

"When?"

Beau waved his hand somewhat ambiguously. At first Antonio couldn't decipher what he was saying. Then he figured it out:

"Many strokes?"

Beau nodded in the affirmative.

"Uncle Beau, can you speak at all?"

Beau nodded in the negative.

Antonio turned to the Clerk. "Please, get Judge Nakamura in here and keep the jury out."

Nakamura took the bench outside the presence of the jury. "What is going on here?"

"Your Honor. My client cannot communicate, other than to nod his head 'yes' and 'no.' But I think he has communicated to me that he has had a number of strokes."

Nakamura looked at Antonio with surprise and concern: "Mr. Browne-Katich, you have been this man's lawyer for four years now. Are you telling me that you haven't figured out that your client is unable to speak until just now?"

Antonio felt embarrassment, mortification and desperation. "Your Honor, now that you mention it, my uncle -- excuse me, my client-- has been speaking less and less for quite a long time. But he has always been able to communicate with me. He testified in his last trial. Yes, he passed out on the witness stand at the end of his testimony. Even so, I thought he was able to testify in this one. No doctor has examined him since his arrest to my knowledge."

"Not even at USP Leavenworth?"

"As I said, your Honor, not to my knowledge."

"When did you last speak with your uncle – excuse me, your client?"

Antonio's heart sank. "I haven't spoken with him in three years."

Nakamura reacted with shock. "Three years! You have been representing this man for four years now, and you haven't spoken with him for the last three of them?"

Antonio's day as the greatest lawyer in America had just ended.

"Your Honor, I...I...I feel so terrible about this. You see, after Mr. Browne was convicted and sent to Leavenworth, he made it very clear that he didn't want to speak to anybody. He would only communicate by e-mail and typewritten message. I honored Mr. Browne's wish, and so did my sister, Mr. Browne's wife and his children. It never occurred to any of us that the reason he did that was because he couldn't speak! And I didn't specifically meet with Mr. Browne this past month, because we had already tried this case once, and I knew everything about this case that I thought I needed to know. Everything, as it turns out, except the most important thing: How is my client doing?"

The new prosecutor interrupted. "May I say something? If this man can communicate 'yes' and 'no,' then he understands what is going on. And his lawyer obviously doesn't need to hear details from this man, since this is the second trial. I suggest you declare him competent and move on."

That argument may well have worked with Hixson or with Mendez. It didn't work with Nakamura.

"No. Someone who is not capable of communicating a message other than 'yes,' or 'no' is not capable of communicating effectively. I will accept the proposition that Beau Browne understands the charges against him. But I am not prepared to accept the proposition that he is able to assist in his defense. I want this man examined by a neurologist, a forensic psychiatrist and a neuropsychologist. I want their input into whether this man is now competent to stand trial. I will excuse the jury today and bring them back tomorrow afternoon. In the meantime, I order the Government to get those three professionals to examine this man ASAP, certainly no later than tomorrow morning, and report to me on this Defendant's competence to stand trial. If in the medical opinion of these professionals this Defendant needs to be hospitalized for testing and diagnosis, I order the US Marshal to transport him to the nearby hospital for that purpose, and I will continue the hearing and the trial if need be until the three professionals are prepared to testify."

Antonio was horrified at what happened. But the ramifications of his neglect of his client had just begun.

The next afternoon, the neurologist, the forensic psychiatrist and the neuropsychologist arrived with their opinions: Based on the MRIs and the examination of the film, as well, as the battery of neuropsychological testing, Beau Browne had suffered no less than 30 vascular and lacunar strokes. For that reason, Pastor Browne could not physically speak.

In horror, Antonio asked the neurologist, "Doctor, can you tell from the MRIs when the first stroke might have been?"

The neurologist replied, "It is old. That's about all I can say. In fact, there are a good number that are old."

Antonio asked the next question, scared of the answer: "Doctor, is it possible that Pastor Browne suffered his first stroke as long ago as January 23, 2051."

The doctor replied, "It's very possible."

And then Beau Browne tugged on Antonio's sleeve. He stuck his thumb up. And Antonio had his answer:

Not merely 'possible'; yes. The first stroke happened when Gloom and Doom water boarded Pastor Browne. The FBI did this to Uncle Beau.

Antonio continued: "Doctor, is it possible that Pastor Browne suffered two more strokes in December of 2051 during his trial, one when he saw the US Marshals manhandle his sister-in-law and his attorney in open court, and one when he tried to testify but passed out on the witness stand?"

Again, the doctor replied, "It's very possible."

Again, Beau Browne tugged on Antonio's sleeve and stuck his thumb up.

The FBI did this to Beau Browne, but not just they. Judge Hixson also did this to Beau Browne.

Antonio continued: "Doctor: For that matter, is it possible that Pastor Browne suffered some strokes while in jail back in 2051, and for that reason was willing to plead guilty when he knew he had done nothing wrong, just to avoid the pressure of a jury trial and the specter of even more strokes?"

"Anything is possible, Counselor." But Beau's extended thumb told Antonio that Antonio had finally figured out what really happened prior to trial when Beau told Antonio he would plead guilty.

And finally: "Doctor: Does the medical evidence establish that the most recent stroke happened as soon as yesterday?"

"Yes."

"Is it possible that Pastor Browne suffered a stroke when he took the stand to testify again?"

"From the medical evidence, I can only say that the last stroke happened in the past 24 hours. But yes, that too is very possible."

It wasn't just the FBI and Judge Hixson who did this to Beau Browne. The whole system of federal criminal justice did this to Beau Browne. It had crushed him like a fermented grape.

Judge Nakamura declared Beau Ezekiel Browne to be incompetent to stand trial, and ordered him transported to the most appropriate care center for determination as to whether he could regain his competency. Judge Nakamura also declared a mistrial. Would this case actually see a third trial, after all?

Most of the time when a defendant is found to be incompetent, he is transported to a mental hospital, where he is fed various cocktails of psychotropic drugs until he "magically" understands what the hell is going on and is declared "competent again."

In this case, Pastor Beau Browne ended up in a nursing home, where he died six months later of complications from multiple strokes.

Our government murdered Pastor Beau Ezekiel Browne.

XXVIII

The Congregational Church overflowed with family, friends, funeral onlookers and media. The fire marshal would have had an overtime kind of day with this crowd. Probably 500 people attended, in a church sanctuary that seated 400. And outside on the church lawn, with video remotes, probably thousands more watched, maybe millions. Family, well-wishers, people whose lives Pastor Browne had touched, media from all over the world with remote feeds, and most prominently, people whose lives Pastor Browne's true story had touched, all attended. Beau's widow, Beau's children and grandchildren, Bonita, Antonio, and Ana sat in the front row.

At the end of the organ prelude and the singing of "Amazing Grace," the presiding pastor stood up to speak.

"Dear Friends: We are gathered here together, hundreds of us -- no, hundreds of thousands of us -- in the eyes of the Lord, to pay tribute to Beau Ezekiel Browne. A kind man. An honest man. A devoted husband, father, and uncle. A man with integrity. A man with nothing in his heart but love and compassion for his fellow man. And, contrary to what some in the United States Government choose to believe, a super, duper patriot."

The crowd cheered and stood, applauding. As the applause died down, and as everyone took his or her seat and the pastor resumed speaking, a loud wail interrupted the proceedings:

"Bo! Bo! Bonita! Bo!"

And there at the back of the sanctuary stood Esperanza, dressed all in black with a black veil around her face.

Beau's widow hissed, "What is she doing here? Get her out of here!"

But Bonita stood up. And by instinct she held out one hand tentatively. She then straightened that arm, held out the other arm, and said nothing.

Esperanza ran to her wife, wrapped her arms around her, and bawled. She just bawled. And through her tears, she had one and only one thing to say: "I'm sorry. I'm just so very sorry." She repeated those words at least ten times, while literally the whole world watched.

The presiding pastor kindly said, "I'm sure you two would like to discuss your private affairs away from the fire marshal, who may be arriving around the corner any second now!"

The funeral attendees broke the tension and laughed nervously, while Bonita and Esperanza walked arm-in-arm down the aisle of the sanctuary toward the exit. Halfway down, Antonio got up and ran to join them. And Ana then got up and ran to join her husband.

Outside, the two women held each other and just cried, Esperanza more loudly than Bonita. Esperanza simply repeated, "Just so very sorry." This woman, who had made millions of dollars during her lifetime with her words, had nothing else to say but "Just so very sorry."

Ana turned to her husband and said, "Antonio, I think it's most important that you go back in there and give your eulogy for your Uncle Beau. I will stay here with your mother and your momma." She kissed her husband, and Antonio dutifully went back into the sanctuary to his assigned seat.

Ana thought: *When she says 'Just so very sorry,' does she mean that she is sorry for all of the grief and pain that she has caused her wife and her son, or is she sorry for herself? I will find out:*

As the two women stood there, holding each other and softly sobbing, Ana said to Esperanza, "It does not matter who you are or what you are, or who you believe or what you believe. If you are truly sorry, if you truly admit that you have made serious mistakes and there is nothing left for you to do but to try to make it right, God will forgive you. He will. He will forgive you."

Esperanza turned to her daughter-in-law, reached out, hugged her, and through her tears said in a choked-up voice, "Thank you, Ana. Thank you."

Ana Katich from America had her answer.

The three women stood there like that, outside on the lawn of the Congregational Church, holding each other. However important the funeral of Beau Browne in the inside of the church was to the rest of the world, nothing was more important in that moment than to hold each other, and to say, "I'm sorry," "Thank you," and ultimately, "I love you."

Finally, Bonita said, "I think it's time to come home."

Esperanza asked in a whisper, "Can I come home?"

And Bonita responded, channeling her mother and caressing her lover: "*Por supuesto.*"

In that moment, Antonio, having just finished his eulogy, came out to join the three women.

"Is everything all right here?"

Bonita and Esperanza were crying too loudly to speak. Ana took her husband's hand, looked lovingly at him, and kissed him. "Everything is fine."

As the crowd emptied out of the church, the family got into their cars for the drive to the graveyard and the burial. Esperanza unlocked and opened the passenger side door of her driverless car, and sat down. She was about to start the keyless ignition, when she looked in the armrest on the passenger door.

There in the slot of the armrest she saw two pennies.

She picked them up with a puzzled expression on her face. Who put those there? She thought about it for a bit. Pennies hadn't been in mainstream currency, since money went almost paperless and the Government ceased the coinage of pennies twenty-five years ago. Nobody else had been in that seat in, well, how long now? She hadn't loaned the car to anybody. Where on earth did those pennies come from?

Esperanza put the two pennies into her purse, not giving the moment a second thought, other than "five pennies will make a nickel."

XXIX

Six months later, Antonio Browne-Katich came home from his new job as an Assistant Federal Public Defender. He opened the door to his apartment and said hello to his pregnant wife.

Ana Katich, with a very intense expression on her face, said, "Antonio. You will never believe what we just got in the mail today."

"What?"

"Here, read it out loud."

The letter, addressed to Antonio Browne-Katich and to Ana Katich, read as follows:

"Dear Antonio and Ana:

As you undoubtedly know by now, Congress recently voted to repeal the Super Patriot Act of 2049. What you may not have known is that when the President of the United States was assured that Congress would do that, he granted me a full and unconditional pardon, and I was released from prison.

The media has made Sonny Stix the hero of this, for all of the money he has poured into the action to repeal this law. And certainly, the media points to the efforts of Deacon Joe Green and of Professor Fred Dockett before that, in order to make it happen.

But I don't consider those three to be the only heroes. I have heard the stories of what you two did to help make it happen. I know of the efforts you two made, on behalf of Pastor Browne, in bringing this unjust law to its rightful knees. I wish I could have met your uncle, Antonio, so that I could have told him this myself. Alas, it was not to be. So please consider this letter as my belated attempt to do so.

I am certain that your uncle did the right thing, just as I know I did. I am also certain that law enforcement's zealousness in enforcing this unjust law is what killed your uncle. But it did not kill me. A famous German philosopher, Friedrich Nietzsche, once said, 'That which does not kill me makes me stronger.' In my case, that is true. With this law repealed and with me able to resume my work, I will be stronger.

I must be stronger. My time in prison has made me realize that the people of America have fooled themselves over the past sixty years. In the guise of loving their country and professing to be Christians, they have abandoned their Christian beliefs and have made this country weaker.

But history is about cycles. I, for one, believe that the past seventy-five years have been a 'dark age' in American history, and our 'dark age' is done.

I am ready to do my part in making this country stronger, just as I am sure you are ready to do yours. Let us go together, follow Christ's basic principles, love, tolerate and understand each other, wage love and not war, and be strong. Together.

In God's love,
Dennis Monroe
Bishop, First United Methodist Church, Fort Worth, Texas"

About the Author

Rick Cornell, born on June 9, 1952 in Pittsburgh, Pennsylvania, is an emerging author in the area of mystery and suspense - legal fiction/courtroom drama. He began practicing law after being admitted to the California Bar in 1977, then moved to Nevada and, after a two-year federal clerkship, began practicing in Nevada in 1980. His practice has morphed into an appeals and writs practice, mostly criminal but some family law. He lives in Reno, Nevada, where his other great passion in life is opera and jazz singing.